AF006414

Secret Service Mandate 7266, otherwise known as the Ogmios Directive, sanctioned the formation of an elite team under the command of Sir Charles Wyndham. Their orders are to do anything and everything necessary to preserve the sovereignty of the British Isles. What that actually means is difficult to pin down. They are deniable. They act outside the law, removed from the security of the State.

If something went wrong they were on their own.

If something went right no one ever said thank you.

It was enough that when things went to hell, they were there. Sir Charles, known affectionately to his people as the old man, calls them the Forge Team, but their nickname amongst themselves is the Lost Cause.

They serve at the pleasure of Her Majesty and report to a faceless bureaucrat in the upper echelons of government known only as Control, though no one with the power to would ever admit that.

These five men and women are often the last hope.

WARGOD

BOOK FOUR OF

THE OGMIOS DIRECTIVE

STEVEN SAVILE
AND SEAN ELLIS

Proudly published by Snowbooks

Copyright © 2017 Steven Savile & Sean Ellis

Steven Savile and Sean Ellis assert the moral right to be identified as the authors of this work. All rights reserved.

Snowbooks Ltd | email: info@snowbooks.com
www.snowbooks.com.

British Library Cataloguing in Publication Data. A catalogue record for this book is available from the British Library. Paperback / softback

ISBN: 978-1-911390-16-9

First published March 2017

ONE
AFTER THE IDES

Then, Cingulum, Italy — 44 BCE

A great man has died.
Titus Atius Labienus wasn't really sure how he felt about that.

He rose stiffly from his chair, catching the edge of the *XII scripta* board with his hip, and crossed to where his son stood. Quintus was still panting, out of breath because of his sprint from the stables. Excitement and dread burned in his eyes. He grabbed the boy by the shoulders. "They left his body on the floor of the Senate. The conspirators, led by Senator Brutus, then proceeded to the Capitol, crying out as they went: *'People of Rome, we are once again free!'*"

"And? Tell me boy, what happened? Do not leave out a single thing. How did the people take it?"

"Silence. The streets were empty. The citizens fled to their homes and locked themselves within."

Labienus chewed on the inside of his lip, mind racing. He released his grip on the boy's shoulders and turned away. *A great man has died and those who would take his place lack even a measure of his greatness.* "Caesar was beloved of the mob. Did the fools imagine they would be glorified for such treachery?"

Quintus cast a glance at the other man seated at the game table. Marcus Atrius, a centurion from one of Caesar's loyal legions, a cavalry commander, and Labienus' gaoler. He remained motionless. The soldier didn't even meet Quintus' gaze. With as much neutrality as he could muster, the young man said. "The aristocracy celebrates behind their closed doors."

Labienus waved a hand dismissively. "You think? Then you are a bigger fool than they are."

Quintus continued to eye the centurion, not sure what to expect from the man of violence. He weighed every word carefully. "Labienus, was not Gaius Julius Caesar your enemy? Now that he is dead, you can appeal to the Senate to end your house arrest."

"Friend, enemy. Sometimes these are one and the same. I was loyal to a great man. I was friends with a great man. And when the time came, I stood against a great man. Does that make us enemies? I was Caesar's foremost lieutenant in Gaul and Britannia. We were as brothers then." Labienus' voice grew almost wistful with the reminiscence, but then his tone shifted and became hard as diamond. "You misapprehend my meaning, boy. They are not fools for having killed him. They are fools because they believe themselves ready for such treason. They are not ready for what must happen next."

Quintus gazed back intently, as if this was something he had not considered. "What *will* happen next?"

"Brutus is not strong enough to control the Senate, much less rule Rome in their name. The mob *worshipped* Caesar, and they will be looking for someone to take his place..."

Quintus did not notice the change in the father's demeanour. "Caesar named Octavian his heir, but he is young, and many think him too weak to rule. Antony has the army—"

"Antony, Brutus…and a dozen more pretenders will rise. There will be a bloody struggle for power, and the people will be the ones to suffer as Rome bathes in yet another civil war. A great man has died, a god among men, and none of those who would assume his place will ever possess anything approaching his greatness." Labienus offered a tight smile and clapped his son's shoulder. "Leave me now, boy. I would think on your news. We can talk more of this on the morrow."

Quintus nodded and, after clasping his father's hand, exited the terrace.

Labienus turned to the centurion. To his credit, the legionary had not reacted to Quintus' news, but he could not completely hide his shock. The old man turned to him. "What will you do now, Marcus?" Labienus asked.

"I do not believe it." The centurion shook his head. Suspicion began to ferment in his eyes. "This is a trick. Some game of yours. Your son seeks to deceive me."

"To what purpose? Have I chafed under the terms of Caesar's judgment? Have I tried to slip these bonds of captivity?" Labienus softened his tone. "You are my gaoler, true, but more than that, you are my friend, Marcus. My brother-in-arms. You know me. You know that I would never attempt so vulgar a deception."

"So then it is a false report. Your own death has been widely reported."

Labienus shrugged slightly. "True, my friend, and the truth is ever a slippery beast when it comes to Rome. It will soon be known, though. If Caesar is murdered, my boy won't be the only one bringing such ill news to our door. But by then, it may already be too late."

Marcus nodded absently then jerked his head up suddenly suspicious. "Too late? For what?"

"To choose a side, brother." Labienus sagged into a chair across from Marcus. "Where are your loyalties?"

"I—I serve Rome."

"As did I, when Caesar crossed the Rubicon. That is why I stood with Pompey." He shook his head. "What is best for Rome and the future that awaits her may not be the same thing. You will have to decide, and then stand by your decision."

Marcus thought about this. "Octavian is the rightful heir," he said. "If Caesar has indeed been assassinated, then my loyalty must lie with Octavian."

"And if Octavian is not strong enough? What then? Would you serve a weak and venal Emperor?"

"His strength will depend upon the loyalty of his commanders. He has my loyalty. I do not know what more I can do."

Labienus regarded the centurion thoughtfully. Loyalty. Julius Caesar inspired such loyalty. But for Octavian, young and unproven, the loyalty of men like Marcus Atrius would not be guaranteed. At the first sign of weakness, they would desert him, or more likely, assassinate him.

He leaned forward and idly picked up the dice from the *scriptus* board. "Remind me. Were you with us for the campaign in Britain, Marcus?"

"Your memory has deserted you, Titus. We were unable to make the crossing. My cohort was on one of the ships that returned to Gaul."

Labienus nodded absently. The question had been rhetorical, and even if the centurion had answered in the affirmative, Labienus was quite sure that the cavalryman had no knowledge of the tale he was about to tell.

*

From one moment to the next, everything changed.

The sun, glinting off the river, the shallow water frothing against the ankles of the infantry as they began fording, the rhythmic crunch of hundreds of pairs of feet, all marching in unison....

And then, chaos.

As the legionaries began the crossing, the Britons commenced their assault. Arrows and stones lashed through the air, clashed against shields, and too often crunched into flesh and bone.

The formation held.

For a few minutes.

The shields repelled the incoming missiles and the advance continued. But then, as the infantrymen neared the eastern shore, a war cry rose up from behind the fortification of pointed stakes and the barbarians streamed out to meet them while they were still knee deep in the water. Roman steel struck iron in a clangour of noise and spray. The unified voice of the war cry became a discordant wail of pain as blades and lances tore through armour to cleave limbs and spill entrails. A stench filled the air, the smell of blood and death.

Labienus knew that every battle started this way. No amount of training could completely prepare a soldier for those first few moments of violence. Nevertheless, those who survived the initial clash knew the critical importance of discipline in the face of death. Today would be no exception.

He urged his mount forward, into the river, exhorting the centurions to close ranks and stay in formation.

Discipline would keep them alive.

The legionaries came together, shields forming a mobile wall bristling with spears. They continued their relentless advance.

Labienus glanced back and found Caesar, riding forward at a slow trot, only a few steps away from the *aquilifer* who held the gleaming eagle standard of the legion high for all to see. The consul of Gaul sat tall astride his mount, one hand resting on the hilt of his sheathed *gladius*. He looked confident and charismatic. He was meant to. The men looked to him as the blood spilled. They wanted to see a hero. He was the nearest thing to a living god—Hercules reborn—and his legions would willingly follow him into the Underworld itself.

And without me, *Labienus thought,* that's exactly where they would all end up.

Caesar was indeed an inspirational figure, to say nothing of a brilliant statesman, an expert swordsman, a scholar, a philosopher, man of the people…but he was no tactician. That was Labienus' job. Labienus won the wars, and Caesar basked in the glory.

Labienus harboured no resentment or jealousy. He well understood the importance of symbols. The legionaries were formidable, not because the troops were brutalized with threats or bribed with promised rewards, but because they each recognised that by winning the battle, they would share in Caesar's glory. That, Labienus knew, was even more essential to victory than rigorous training, the superior weapons and his tactics. The moment any battle was joined, strategy became a thing of the past, for the command tent. War was like a river, relentless, fluid, always moving, surging around the combatants, constantly changing itself to sweep away any obstacle. And someone like Caesar was a rock. Immovable.

Mandubracias rode next to him, watching the battle with an expression that was both eager and rueful. Labienus didn't like the man, but the battlefield was no place for niceties. You could not choose your allies in battle any more than you chose your enemies. The sky was grey and overcast, a thick mist rising up from the long grass. Briton was a godforsaken land. He missed the gods' own country. Mandubracias, the prince of the Trinovantes—the largest and most powerful tribe in Britain—had been driven from the island by a fierce war leader from the neighbouring Catuvellauni tribe—a man named Cassivelaunus—who had hounded his every step, mercilessly meeting him on every field of battle and leaving him with only food for the island's ravens and crows, before Mandubracias had given up and sought refuge in Gaul. The man was a coward. He'd come running with his tail between his legs, begging for help from their new Roman allies.

Determined to show the Britons that Rome took care of her friends, Caesar spent the winter building ships to ferry his legions across the channel, and with the coming of spring, launched an invasion the like of which the Island of the Mighty hadn't seen.

The immortals are capricious. The Venti and Neptune himself conspired against the ships, the seas rising as the winds whipped them up, damaging the ships, shearing timbers and splitting bows, forcing them back to Gaul.

Nevertheless, Caesar was supremely confident of victory. He had made offerings to Bellona, Nerio, Mars and Minerva. He had read the omens. He did not lose. And he would not lose now. Labienus was confident, too, though his enthusiasm for the battle was tempered by the lessons of experience. Once the battle was joined, anything could happen. He did not trust the Britons. Cassivelaunus' warriors were relatively inexperienced, but they were fighting on familiar terrain. Mandubracias had proved to be an invaluable source of information about both the landscape and the tactics the Catuvellauni would likely employ, but Labienus remained wary of the prince; where would his sympathies lie when Roman soldiers started slaughtering Britons?

A cry arose from behind Labienus.

A skirmish broke out on the west side of the river, where a contingent of Welsh warriors rushed from concealment and charged headlong into the centre of the marching column. Swords clashed against shields and blades as the war cries became shrieks. The ground beneath their feet was treacherous, thick with mud from heavy rains.

"Nennius," Mandubracias growled, seeing the brother of his hated foe, Cassivelaunus. "So, that dog leads them? Then let us teach the whelp some lessons, shall we?"

Forty men clothed in the forest itself surged forward, yelling as though trying to raise the demons of Britain to fight at their side.

The surprise attack was bold, but Nennius' force was too small to inflict any meaningful damage on the Roman infantry, no matter how courageous the Britons at his command were, or how desperate. The infantry simply closed ranks.

Labienus watched the slaughter.

He was a tactician to the bone. There was nothing random in a first strike. The ambush would have been devastating if Nennius had waited a while longer and struck at the rear of the column, but something had the Briton attack when and where he did. And there was only one thing Labienus could think of: Nennius was trying to reach Caesar.

Fall back, Labienus willed, as though the War God might somehow hear the words spoken in his own mind.

There were too many ways to die on the battlefield, and while the death of scores or even hundreds of legionaries was an acceptable price for victory, the death of one man could mean total defeat, if that man was Gaius Julius Caesar.

But he knew Caesar. He would not retreat in the face of a threat. As important as it was for the leader of the Roman armies to stay alive, it was imperative that he never give the appearance of fear. His power as an icon would quickly rot if rumours of cowardice ever began to circulate. The tactician watched with a mixture of dread and certainty as Caesar turned his horse toward the fray and drew his *gladius* from its scabbard. It wasn't about appearance now. The heat of the battle was rising and the simple truth was that the man *enjoyed* this; he craved battle. He savoured the fight, relished testing himself, and the stronger the foe, the better. But most of all, he lived for the glory of victory.

Caesar thrust the *gladius* skyward like a threat to the heavens themselves, and spun it above his head, the gleaming metal catching a glint of sunlight. For just a moment, a single solitary heartbeat, it looked like a pillar of golden fire above his head. The effect was spectacular. Caesar was more than just an ordinary man.

Then, to Labienus' dismay, Caesar swung down from his mount and charged into the fray on foot.

It was madness!

Breathing a curse, Labienus turned his horse and charged toward the melee. He wasn't about to let the War God prove his mortality.

Caesar's sword arced back and forth, hewing a path through the Britons. The sword cleaved iron armour, wooden shields, and human limbs alike, slick with blood and glittering in the rising sun. Caesar barely seemed to break his stride. He met each foe head-on, and dispatched them with ruthless efficiency. He really was more than human.

Before Labienus could cross half the distance, Caesar had reached Nennius.

The two men met in a clash of iron and steel.

Sunlight danced like flames on the edge of the Roman leader's sword. It was a stark contrast to the dull reddish-grey iron of the Briton's blade.

Both men moved with the grace of killers.

Both men moved with the precision of survivors.

Labienus yelled a warning, but it was lost beneath the fury of the battle.

Caesar swung.

Nennius staggered back as Caesar's sword hammered into his own.

The young man tried to raise his blade to parry another punishing blow, and barely succeeded. Caesar's blade slid along the upraised sword and struck a glancing blow to the side of the prince's head. Nennius' helmet saved his life. It was torn free by the impact, exposing matted, flaxen hair and a wound that streamed scarlet down his face. The prince staggered away, disoriented, and Caesar drew back for a final swing.

At least it will be over quickly, *Labienus thought.*

And then the unexpected happened.

The gods laughed at them.

As Caesar brought the sword down, Nennius somehow succeeded in getting his shield up to catch the blow. The

Roman's sword cleaved the wood, splitting it down to the iron bands that held it together. It stuck fast. Caesar fought desperately to wrench the sword free, but in the same instant, Nennius hauled back savagely on the shield, and the mud beneath their feet betrayed them. As both men stumbled, Labienus was stunned to see that the sword had been torn from Caesar's grasp.

Time on the battlefield held, one second becoming one minute as both Nennius and Caesar seemed unable to grasp what had just happened.

Caesar stared at his empty hands, slick with the blood of fallen enemies, while Nennius gazed over the top of his shield, waiting for Caesar to finally deliver the killing blow. Then realization dawned. Nennius lowered his shield and wrapped his fingers around the hilt of Caesar's sword.

"Protect Caesar!" Labienus screamed, spurring his horse forward, crossing the ground at a gallop.

Nennius ripped the sword free of the shield, a sneer on his battle-scarred face, and held up Crocea Mors, Caesar's *gladius*, triumphantly. "Now, you die," he said, then loosed a harsh cry of exultation. His eyes gleamed with renewed vigour. He would not die. Not now. Not here. The Briton advanced on his unarmed foe.

Half a dozen legionaries, responding to Labienus' battle cry, shifted formation to make a protective wall around Caesar, blocking Nennius' path to the War God.

Without shield or helm, and still reeling from the head blow, the prince seemed little match for these battle-hardened legionnaires, but the young warrior trod relentlessly forward, and when the first of the soldiers tried to attack, he was ready. The captured sword flashed out, and the Roman before him fell in an arc of arterial blood. Another went down; his body toppling over like a fallen tree, to lie beside his severed head.

The carrion birds would feed well that day, no matter what happened next.

The Britons rallied at the sight of their leader's heroics, and suddenly, what had been a skirmish verged on a catastrophic rout for the Romans.

Nennius continued cleaving through the wall of Romans, cutting good men down and moving faster than Caesar's protectors could retreat with their charge.

Labienus angled his horse toward Nennius, but before he could add his own sword to the fray, a sling-shot stone cast from the midst of the enemy horde struck the animal squarely in the skull. It went down in a tangle of limbs, and Labienus was pitched headlong, his sword lost to him in the fall.

He hit the ground hard. Through the cloud of pain, Labienus was aware of just how vulnerable he was, lying there sprawled out like a whore in the mud. He struggled to rise, and fumbled for the hilt of his sword. Through the mask of mud that clung to his face, he saw death come striding towards him in the guise of Nennius.

The Briton raised the gleaming *gladius*.

Still on his knees, Labienus wrestled with his own sword, struggling to drag it free of its scabbard. He barely managed to raise it as the young prince brought Caesar's blade scything down at him, parrying it. The impact sent him sprawling flat on his back. A shock of pain lanced up his forearm. He lost his grip on the hilt of his sword as his nerveless fingers sprang open. The blade spilled from his hand.

Nennius recovered quickly.

He raised the captured blade for another attack.

A strange numbness flooded through the Roman; it was death advancing. The dawning realisation that there wasn't a single thing he could do to prevent the sword from sweeping down to cleave his body open. But some animal part of him refused to die. Fate was not written. It was made. He rolled to his side and reached out, desperately clawing at the mud for the hilt of the fallen sword. His fingers caught the wrapping. His grip was clumsy; his hand felt like so much dead meat attached to his wrist; but with every ounce of will left to him, Labienus brought the steel blade up to deflect Nennius' killing blow.

The *gladius* came down and the blades rang together for an instant, and then the tone shifted, no longer singing the song of battle. The final note fell flat as Labienus' blade snapped in two.

The blade of the broken sword spun away as a fresh wave of agony surged up all the way to his shoulders, but the sensation was mercifully brief. He tried desperately to fend off the next blow with nothing more than the hilt of the sword, but Nennius' blade slipped easily past it and hammered into the side of Labienus' helmeted head.

The Roman warrior saw darkness, and beyond it, thought he saw Elysium.

*

"Nennius killed fourteen men with that sword. Fourteen. Every single man that stood against him and felt the touch of that blade died."

"Except you," Marcus observed dryly. "But then, you always were too cantankerous to be allowed entry to Elysium. I'm not surprised they sent you back to the land of the living."

Labienus smiled patiently. "The Britons believed that Nennius had slain me, so as far as they were concerned, I died on that field. I awoke two days later in the care of Caesar's physicians. It was a month before I was able to stand.

"Nennius' victory counted for little in the grand scheme of things, of course; it didn't even slow us down. The legionaries were relentless. They advanced, driving on until he was forced to flee. The land was ours. Our army forded the river and scattered the Britons. Nennius himself died ten days later, a victim of the wound Caesar inflicted before losing that damned blade.

"The Britons, like all of their Celtic ancestors, live and breathe superstition. They are simple-minded. They believe in wraiths and vengeful spirits, and bury their dead in barrows inside the earth, equipping them with grave goods for the afterlife. Nennius was entombed near their settlement, Caesar's sword buried with him. The Britons believed it was a thing of power. They called it 'yellow death,' because of the way it shone with golden light on the battlefield. As I said, they are simple people."

Marcus leaned forward. "Why are you telling me this?"

Labienus gave a grim smile, but did not answer directly. "Did you know that before he became a leader of armies, Julius Caesar was a candidate to become the high priest of Jupiter?"

The centurion shook his head. "No. And none of the tales I have heard about him include that 'fact'."

"A political reversal stripped him of that destiny. He chose to become a soldier. When he left Rome, he carried that sword with him. It was a sacred relic from the Temple of Jupiter, which he took when the temple was destroyed during Sulla's wars. It was reputed to be the sword of Mars himself, forged by Vulcan, and possessed of divine power. Venus bequeathed it to Aeneas, who in turn brought it to Rome."

"And you said the Britons were the superstitious fools," Marcus scoffed.

Labienus raised an eyebrow. "One does not preclude the other, my friend. I am not about to pretend to know the truth. The sword may well possess unearthly properties; equally, it may not. I cannot say, but think on this: with that sword, Caesar carved out an even greater destiny for himself than the priesthood."

"And that makes it magical? There is a flaw in your reasoning, old man. The sword was lost long before he became the dictator of Rome."

Labienus nodded. "Ah, indeed it was. But that is only ever part of the story. An aspect. When I learned of Nennius' death, I proposed leading an assault on the Briton stronghold to retrieve the blade from the prince's tomb. Caesar refused my request. 'It is only a sword,' he told me. 'If I take it back from them, they will believe it is the sword that has conquered them, not the man who wields it.' And of course, he was correct. He did not need the sword to defeat Cassivelaunus, nor to take Rome."

"Then I ask again, why are you telling me this?"

Labienus let him think about it for a moment, and then said: "The sword of Julius Caesar would be a powerful symbol for anyone standing in his place, don't you think?"

Understanding dawned on the centurion's face. "Whoever holds that sword...he would be more than just Caesar's heir. He would be chosen by the gods."

"Now you understand why I have told you this old story of mine again."

"But who is worthy of that honour? Octavian? Marc Antony?"

"As Caesar said, it is only a sword. A symbol. Important in and of itself, but only a symbol. More important is the character of the man chosen to wield it." Labienus leaned back in his chair and waved a hand. "Of course, given the fact that the sword is not in our possession, this entire conversation is a little presumptuous."

"Where is it?"

"Right where it has been these ten years: with Nennius, in his tomb, in Briton."

Marcus stood up abruptly, his features taut with purpose. "Then that is where we must go."

Labienus smiled. "That is where we must go."

PART ONE
EMPIRE

TWO
BROTHERS IN ARMS

Now, London — 1955 UTC (Universal Time, Coordinated)

Ronan Frost easily picked out the two men from the mass of people idling along the narrow pavement of Kensington High Street, looking in the shop windows and pretending to belong.

There was nothing particularly remarkable about them.

They wore blue jeans and anoraks over bright red Arsenal tee-shirts. Short hair, but not too short; rough features, but not too rough...unremarkable.

He spotted the first of the pair lounging on a plastic bus stop bench in front of the Royal Garden Hotel. The man was reading a copy of *The Sun*. His eyes came up every few seconds to sweep the street. His head never moved. The second man leaned against the wrought-iron fence near the park entrance a hundred metres further down, smoking a cigarette and watching people come and go. Trying too hard to be inconspicuous and blend into the background. Frost immediately pegged them as watchers.

Amateurs, he thought; but that was what bothered him.

Had he been meant to notice them? Were they a distraction to throw him off balance? Were there others following him? Ones who knew what he'd look for and were therefore more adept at escaping his notice?

I'm overthinking this, he decided. But sometimes, that was good. He thought about the phone call that had summoned him.

"Someone just tried to kill me," Tony Denison had said before Frost could even digest the fact that a ghost had called him. They'd kept in contact for a while after Frost's selection for the SAS, but their lives had taken different paths, and they were guys, so it wasn't like they sent Christmas cards and birthday wishes. The first thing Frost had thought on hearing Denison's voice after all this time was: 'Why?' His second thought had been: 'Why me?'

The answer to the latter was obvious—at least on the surface.

Denison knew better than anyone that Ronan Frost was the kind of guy you wanted watching your back. They'd served together in 1 PARA—Denison a Lieutenant Colonel and battalion commander, Frost an infantry sergeant. Denison had given him the nickname 'Robin,' like Del Boy's car, the Reliant Robin, because old Reliable Ronan never let you down. It could have been worse, all things considered. But it deflected attention from his Irish heritage, and among a group of men whose collective, inherited memory of Bloody Sunday was just a bit different than what the history books said. Robin: disciplined, impeccable, unflappable, drama-free, deadly. That was who and what he was. That was why he'd been such a damn good soldier, and why he'd eventually wound up working for Sir Charles Wyndham as part of his Ogmios Team—the blackest of black ops.

Denison couldn't know about that last bit, but he absolutely knew the rest.

"Someone just tried to kill me," he'd said, his laboured breathing audible in Frost's Bluetooth earbud.

"Hang up and call the police."

"No. Can't trust the police. I don't know who to trust." *Except for you*; he didn't have to say that bit.

After Kosovo—after Frost had left for the SAS—Denison had risen, almost effortlessly, to the rank of Brigadier. But then his military career had stalled. A vocal critic of Blair's support for the United States' adventure in Iraq—he'd been quoted as calling it "the worst sort of collusion with the devil"—Denison had retired and gone to work for some kind of policy think tank. He'd written a couple of damning books, and was always popping up on Sky News to drive another nail into Blair's political coffin, but beside being a talking-head, there was nothing that would explain why he was the subject of a death mark.

"I was attacked in the car park. I gave him the slip...I think."

"Where are you now?"

"I ran. Safety in visibility."

"Where are you now?" Frost had repeated, enunciating each word in an effort to both calm Denison and get him to focus.

"Kensington High Street, just across from the Royal Gardens. I'm at a Starbucks, sitting in the back."

Bloody Starbucks. He knew it. It was a small hole-in-the-wall coffee shop, with maybe twenty seats inside. Dark from the outside. It was a decent choice. "Don't move. I'm on my way." He'd grabbed the shoulder holster rig which held his Browning Hi-Power 9mm and two spare magazines, donned his leather motorcycle jacket and headed for the door.

On the way out he called Lethe.

Jude Lethe was the man behind the curtain; Sir Charles' technical wizard. He was arguably the most important member of the team. He was certainly irreplaceable. Frost and the others were just the muscle, going where, doing what and killing whomever they were told. But Lethe—navigating his computer network like a conductor leading an orchestra, accessing CCTV feeds and real-time satellite imagery, hacking into whatever needed hacked, laying down false trails and masking real ones—was the brain that guided their deadly efforts.

Frost needed to know why someone wanted Tony Denison dead.

Lethe was the best hope he had of finding out fast.

A heavy backbeat was the first thing Frost had heard as the connection was made.

"Frosty?" Lethe's reedy shout was barely audible.

"Lethe. Turn down the music and listen. I need you to look into something for me."

"You'll have to speak up, fella," Lethe replied. "I can't hear you over the music. Top tune this, by the way. Really gets into your bones."

Frost growled and repeated himself.

"Let me try to get outside. Stay on the line."

Frost sighed.

Outside? Frost had always assumed that Lethe spent every waking minute chained to his desk in Nonesuch Manor—and probably the sleeping minutes, too—working his cyber-magic for the team during on-duty hours, and probably painting his little plastic *Warhammer* figures when off. It hadn't occurred to him that Lethe could have a life outside the Ogmios HQ.

Bollocks. "Never mind," he'd said, and clicked off.

He kept constant pressure on the throttle of his Ducati Monster, matching the flow of evening traffic as he cruised past the Starbucks without a glance, and proceeded to the intersection with Kensington Court. He turned right, and steered to the curb. He pushed back the visor on his helmet and made a casual sweep of the street, making sure he was out of the line of sight for the man at the park gate before ringing Denison's mobile number.

"Robin?"

"More like Batman. I'm here. Just outside. I'm going to come in for a quick recce and an overpriced coffee. Don't react when you see me." When Denison didn't reply, Frost continued. "The man who jumped you; do you see him there?"

"I don't think so. No."

"Good. There are at least two outside. It looks like they sent a team for you. Now I need you to tell me who 'they' are."

"Not over the phone."

"Bloody hell, Tony, what sort of trouble are you in?" Before he could press the issue, a beep in his ear signalled another call coming in. He checked the display on the mobile unit and recognised the number; one of Nonesuch Manor's outside lines. "Just sit tight," he told Denison. "We'll get this sorted."

Without waiting for a response, he tapped the screen to accept the incoming call. "Lethe?"

"No." Sir Charles Wyndham's slightly rheumy voice crackled in his ear. "But as we're presently on stand-down, Mr. Lethe was understandably very concerned to receive an after-hours call and a hang-up."

It wasn't a rebuke, not by any stretch of the imagination, but it stung all the same. Using Ogmios resources for something off the books? Must be serious. Red alert. All hands to the pump. Battle stations. The sky is falling.

"No cause for concern, sir. An old oppo needs some help. I thought I could get our boy wizard to Google something for me."

The old man wasn't buying it. "The fact that your old *oppo* would come looking for the particular brand of help that you specialize in is what interests me. Does he have a name?"

There was no turning back now. If this turned out to be nothing, if Tony Denison was merely trying to dodge a loan collector or the irate husband...well then, he'd be trading in his old pal Robin for Chicken Licken.

Bollocks, he thought. *I can live with that.* "Tony Denison. He was my CO when I was in Kosovo. He thinks someone is trying to kill him. I was hoping Lethe could give me an idea of whom."

"Brigadier Anthony Denison?"

"I prefer to think of him as the toughest old bastard I've worked for—present company excepted."

The old man chuckled. "I make a point of knowing the people that work for me. Denison's name shows up quite a lot in your dossier: commendation letters, recommendation for the Regiment, and so forth. Suffice it to say, if there is a threat to his safety, the full resources of Nonesuch are yours. Lethe is *en route*. When he arrives, I will direct him to commence Googling forthwith."

Frost rang off.

He rounded the corner back onto Kensington High Street and proceeded along the pavement toward the otherwise inconspicuous storefront that bore the stylized siren logo. He scanned the street. The two watchers were still in place, exactly where he'd seen them last. No one else caught his eye.

Two men outside...one more inside? That was how he would have done it. And some sort of proficiency on their side; that one should be much harder to spot.

Frost stepped inside the coffee house.

He checked out the menu board even as he took in the rest of the room with his peripheral vision. He wasn't looking at individual faces but rather, like a real-world variation of a child's find-what-doesn't-belong puzzle, he was looking for what was wrong with the picture. There was no saying what the giveaway might be—the wrong kind of clothes, someone sitting alone, a pair of people more interested in looking around the room than in conversing with each other—and there was no guarantee that the signs, even if he caught them, would identify actual watchers.

"What can I get you, sir?" chirped the girl behind the pastry case.

Frost could play a part. He'd feign indecision, shrug, check out the various muffins, doughnuts, brownies and cinnamon swirls behind the glass, then check the menu one more time, making sure to scan left and right in the process before placing his order for a cappuccino.

"Cappu—" He broke off mid-word—which wasn't exactly subtle—as something he had glimpsed finally registered. Despite all his training and years of experience, despite the knowledge that an uncontrolled reaction might have fatal consequences, Frost very nearly did a double take.

He caught himself before he could blow his cover, and kept his attention firmly on the girl and finishing his order. "No, hell, let's go wild, make it a latte. Double shot."

The girl nodded, smile fixed in place, and busied herself with the ritual coffee prep. Frost was angry with himself.

If there were eyes in the room, he was made. They'd have to have been both deaf and blind not to catch his screw up. He was angry enough to punch something. And right now that anger was focused squarely on his old commanding officer—

who'd just made him look like a chump. He'd made Tony Denison as he'd scanned the room.

Denison wasn't alone.

He was with a woman.

Denison wasn't exactly anonymous. Tall and lanky, stern face, a Roman nose; he was striking, and had an air of authority about him. He wore his black overcoat and a sharp, off-the-rack suit underneath. He was at least ten years older than Frost, but there wasn't a trace of grey in his hair.

But Frost was more interested in the woman.

She was considerably younger than her companion, mid-twenties at a push. High, Slavic cheekbones. Flaxen hair. Not exactly *Tatler* beautiful, but sexy in a high-class hooker kind of way.

His mind churned over the implications.

His first thought was espionage. A honey-trap? But that was a bit elaborate for a retired brigadier. His second thought was much more ordinary, but still driven by sex.

No wonder he didn't want to talk about it over the phone.

Frost took the paper cup with his double-shot latte from the end of the bar and headed for the door. He sipped from the tall cup as he moved, using the opportunity to risk a more thorough scan of the late-night coffee drinkers. Old habits had him assigning each one a nickname based on some distinctive characteristic—a facial feature, hair length, an article of clothing. His gaze did not return to Denison.

Once back outside, he walked to the nearest corner. The smoker was still leaning against the railings outside the Royal Garden. His partner was still at the bus stop. Frost pressed the button on the pedestrian crossing and waited for the green man. He took his mobile out of his pocket, and rang Denison again.

"Who's the girl?"

"Ronan, I—"

Frost heard the reluctance and cut in brusquely. "Cut the crap, Tone. No 'I was going to tell you' rubbish. I can't help you if I don't know what's really going on. I'm going to ask you this once, and you're going to tell me the truth, or I'm going to hang up, walk away and leave you to it. Is she the reason they're after you?"

"Not as such." There was another pause, Denison apparently trying to work out what he could and couldn't say. Then he seemed to grasp what Frost was really asking. "Get your mind out of the gutter, man. It's *nothing* like that. Honestly, I can't explain it over an unsecure line. But no, I can assure you that Lili's role in all of this is tangential at best. She is not the reason I am in trouble."

Lili. The name struck a dim and distant chord in Frost's memory, buried way down deep, but he couldn't connect it to anything concrete. It was just a name. There wasn't time to press the issue. "Here's what you're going to do," he said. "In exactly sixty seconds, you and Lili need to get out of there. Don't look like you're in a hurry, but move with a purpose. Leave by the front door, and go east to the first crossing. Cross the street and head for the park gate. Got it?"

"Sixty seconds," Denison repeated.

Frost hung up and made his way across the street, then headed for the bench with the watcher. He dropped down next to the man with an exaggerated sigh of weariness. The watcher offered a sympathetic nod, and went back to his surveillance.

Frost turned his attention to the storefront across the street, but unlike the man beside him, he wasn't caught off-guard when the familiar figure of Tony Denison, accompanied by the blonde woman, strode through the door. The watcher reacted immediately, his body tensing in anticipation as he rose to his feet.

"Careful," Frost said. Not loud. More of a threat than a warning.

And before the man could react, Frost swept a foot out and took his feet out from under him. In the same motion, he flat-handed a shove between the man's shoulder blades and sent him staggering face-first onto the pavement.

His head cracked loudly as it hit the kerb.

There were half-a-dozen witnesses who would swear that the man had tripped and Frost had tried to catch him. The mind was funny that way; when confronted with a set of unexpected circumstances, people reached for the easiest, and most palatable explanation. That was why eyewitness accounts rarely corresponded perfectly with the physical evidence. A would-be Good Samaritan came towards them, looking to offer what help they could.

Frost wasn't finished.

"Hey, are you all right?" he asked, theatrically as he knelt and slipped a hand around the man's neck. He felt the throb of a carotid pulse against his fingertips as he squeezed. Thirty seconds should do the trick.

His other hand found the pistol tucked in the man's belt at the small of his back. Proof enough he'd not gone soft. He tugged the man's coat down to ensure that no one else saw the gun then looked up at the gathering crowd. "Did you see that? He just went down?"

"Drunk," a sallow-faced snotty-nosed member of the Green Wellie Brigade said dismissively.

Frost nodded knowingly and stood. "Probably. Stay with him, would you? I'll go for help."

And just like that, he was moving again, striding purposefully toward the park entrance and the second watcher. Denison and the woman—Lili—were only a few steps ahead of him on the other side of the thoroughfare.

Frost slowed his pace and scanned the street in both directions. Aside from the man still making a show of casually smoking a filter-tip by the phone box beside the park gate, there was no sign of any back-up. That was either a very good sign, or quite possibly, a very bad one. Paranoia was a safer mind-set than blind optimism, so he assumed the worst, even though there was no evidence to suggest that he was dealing with professionals. Still, until he knew exactly what Denison was mixed up in, he was Mr. Worst Case.

The watcher noticed Denison and Lili crossing the street towards him.

The momentary flicker of recognition as his eyes widened was followed by a poorly disguised effort to remain inconspicuous, even as he readied himself for action. It was almost comically bad.

The watcher made no move as the pair passed him, but as soon as they crossed into the park, he lurched into motion. Frost fell into step behind him, allowing the watcher to outpace, just ever so slightly. The caution was unnecessary. The watcher had developed tunnel vision. He didn't once look away from his quarry. With a copse of trees concealing them from view, the watcher quickened his pace. Frost saw the man reach into the pocket of his coat, going for his gun.

Before it was halfway clear, Frost exploded into action.

He sprinted forward, the Browning drawn but kept low, discreet. The watcher was rigidly eyes-forward. His attention didn't waver. Not even as Frost slammed the butt of the Browning into the back of his skull and took him down.

Frost caught him under the arms and dragged him off the path. "Tony," he rasped.

Twenty metres up the path, Denison turned, his anxiety evident in every muscle of his body as he moved. Frost saw him heave a sigh of relief as he made the motionless form of the watcher. He took Lili's hand and hurried back to where Frost waited.

"You said there were two?"

Frost nodded. "And now there are none. Let's get you somewhere safe. I really want to know what the fuck's going on."

Denison nodded, but Lili quickly jumped in. "There is no time for safe." As Frost had expected, she had a thick Slavic accent. "We must get to Saint Albans, tonight."

"Saint Albans?" Frost kept his gaze on Denison. "Planning a little vacation?"

"No."

"So what's there, then?"

"The answers to everything."

Before Frost could challenge Denison's deliberately cryptic reply, something struck the ground at their feet, digging in with the severity of a hammer blow. It threw up a spray of dirt and grit.

There was no report, meaning the gun was suppressed, but Frost didn't need to hear the *boom* to recognise the impact of a bullet.

Another bullet tore into the greenery.

Frost was no stranger to violence. He'd grown up with the constant awareness of just how quickly a life could be snuffed out. He had come to cherish the surge of adrenaline that accompanied the explosions and incoming gunfire—and he'd learned to compartmentalize his reactions. There was no paralyzing fear, no moment of dumbfounded incomprehension at the realisation that someone was trying to kill him. His military experience had honed his ability to use the physical reaction to his advantage, and like most soldiers, he had an almost fatalistic view of combat: if one of those bullets was meant to end his life, so be it. Soldiers died. It was just what they did.

Nevertheless, self-preservation remained the first order of business.

He reacted instinctively, grabbing Denison with one hand and Lili with the other, pulling them toward the trees. Not that the foliage would offer much cover. As soon as they were down, Frost scanned the path behind them. He glimpsed someone ducking behind another tree, this one about twenty metres away, further from the tell-tale glow of the street lights.

Then a flicker in the shadows caught in his peripheral vision: a second figure moving on the opposite side of the path.

Breathing a curse, Frost leaned in close to the others. "When I start shooting, *run*."

"Where?"

"*Anyfuckingwhere*. It doesn't matter. Just as long as it's away from the bloody bullets."

Denison gave a curt nod, and Frost saw the first glimmer of the old warhorse in his expression. He was going to need that if they were all going to walk out of the park tonight.

One of their assailants made his move.

Frost was ready.

His Browning Hi-Power thundered, shattering the relative quiet of the evening. It didn't sound anything like a car backfiring on Kensington High Street, but that was what bystanders would remember hearing—that, and two rounds smacking into a tree beside the assassin.

Frost ducked back, keeping the bole of the tree between him and the shooters.

Denison and Lili were already sprinting across the grass, abandoning the path for the deeper darkness of the park.

Staying low, he eased away from the tree and waited.

A few seconds later, he heard the crunch of footsteps.

The gunmen were following standard infantry tactics: one man covering the other while moving in a variation of leapfrog. Perfect for taking on an enemy in a static location, but while the two men bounded forward in stages, their real target was racing away. From the moment they'd set foot in the park, Frost's primary objective had been keeping Denison and Lili alive. If he could keep the gunmen occupied a few seconds longer, they'd be off their radar.

Unless there are more of them, Mr. Worst Case thought for him.

In their place, Frost would have wanted to keep the hit team simple. It was reasonable to assume they would work the same way. Always figure the enemy is better than you are. That was a great way to stay alive. The first attempt had been meant to look like a random street crime. This all-out assault smacked of desperation.

He could work with that.

Frost eased out from behind cover and sent a double-tap in the direction of the pair. He wasn't trying to hit them. A gun battle in Kensington Park Garden was the last thing he wanted. And if the hit team had any sense, they would already be melting away into the shadows, disappearing before the police showed up. This wasn't Fallujah. Gunshots didn't go unnoticed.

Without waiting to see their next move, Frost spun on his heel and ran, head down, moving fast, perpendicular to the path, aiming for the edge of the park. As he skirted the wrought-iron barrier that blocked access to the main house, he stowed the Browning and took out his phone to call Denison.

He heard his old friend's laboured breathing over the line. "Ronan?"

"Where are you?"

"The Palace Gate exit. There are other people here. I think they heard the shots."

"That was the point. I think I bought us some breathing room, but you need to keep moving. There's an Underground station a few streets south of here. Buy a ticket to Heathrow."

"The airport?" Frost heard Lili give a small huff of protest. "We can't leave the country, Ronan," Denison continued.

"You're not. It's the fastest way out of here. Forty minutes on the Piccadilly Line, a car rental desk at the other end. I'll make all the arrangements and be waiting for you by the Hertz desk. We'll be in Saint Albans in a couple of hours."

"My car is at the Royal Garden. That's just a street away."

"You need to start thinking, Tony." Frost didn't have the time or the inclination to coddle his old friend. "They attacked you in the car park. They know your car. Even if they think you're too smart to go back for it, they'll have left you a present. You want to be another car bomb statistic, be my guest; but you asked for my help, so how about you do what I say? Take the Tube."

There was a pause and then a reluctant. "You're right. We'll see you there."

Frost pocketed the phone and took a quick look around before heading toward the Palace Gate. Denison would do as instructed. He'd be long gone by the time Frost reached the park exit.

It would be an hour before their paths crossed again. That gave Ronan Frost an hour to work out who was trying to kill Tony Denison, and what was so important about Saint Albans. He walked back to the Monster.

THREE
UNINVITED

2010 UTC

"This is you, no?" The old man thrust a piece of paper under the woman's nose.

She glanced at the scrap, her face screwing up intently as she tried to decipher the scrawl. She had been polite when he'd first spoken to her on the intercom, and had even ventured from her flat to explain the mistake face-to-face, but now her stiff-upper-lip unflappability was reaching breaking point. "No," she said at last, her tone sharp. Condescending. She didn't like the man in front of her. "That's upstairs. I told you. I didn't order any takeaway. You've got the wrong flat."

The old man took the paper back and stared at it. "I tried this, but no one answers. So I think, 'Misha writes numbers wrong.' So I ring you. Are you sure you don't order this? Is *pelmeni*. Is very good. Trust me."

The woman shook her head and pushed the paper away. "Thank you," she said tersely. "I am sure it is wonderful. But no. You'll have to try upstairs again. I'm very sorry, but I can't help you."

"No one answers," the old man repeated. "I think Misha writes wrong address."

"I'm sorry. You need to talk to Misha."

The woman turned away and disappeared back into the building, avoiding eye contact as she hurried back to her first floor apartment.

As the interior door closed, the old man's mask of disappointment fell away, replaced by a satisfied smile. He gave the door a gentle nudge with his foot, having caught it before it could latch behind the woman, and entered the building.

He immediately crossed to the stairwell and shuffled up the steps, clutching the white plastic bag full of Styrofoam food containers as though they contained the crown jewels. As soon as he reached the second floor landing however, he deposited the bag down the rubbish chute and straightened up from his hunched over posture, adding six inches to his height and taking a decade off his age in the process.

Konstantin Khavin moved with the purposefulness of someone who had every right to be there.

He approached one of the doors and placed a hand on the doorknob.

He examined the lock set into the plate just above it: a simple five-pin residential lock. Beyond the exclusive and elaborate electronic locks guarding the main building, the actual locks on the individual doors were laughably inadequate. But that was what security did for you; it gave you a false sense of safety.

He took a slim leather wallet from a pocket and opened it to reveal an array of lock-picking tools, including a locksmith's trigger-activated picking device.

He considered utilising the latter, then decided on a simpler approach.

He selected a filed key blank that matched the lock on the door and slid it home. Though the key did not turn, he maintained steady torque on the head as he deftly pounded on the latch plate. Once, twice, three times. To the residents of the adjacent flats, it would sound like someone knocking, but the vibration of his fists against the door jostled the pins inside the mechanism, causing them to move up and down. On the third blow, the bump key turned and the lock popped open.

Konstantin removed the blank from the lock, and turned the knob, opening the way into Brigadier Tony Denison's Knightsbridge residence.

He had accomplished a lot in the twenty minutes since he'd hung up on Lethe.

The call itself had taken nearly as long, or so it had seemed to Konstantin; Jude Lethe's hyperactive, ironic, terminally hip babble could never be accused of bluntness. The man couldn't find a point if he tried. But the salient fact was: Frost's former commanding officer had become a target for persons currently unknown. Nothing else Lethe had to say mattered.

Like Frost, Khavin was one of Sir Charles Wyndham's Ogmios soldiers, but that was where the similarities ended. Khavin was a spook from an era that existed for the others merely as a paragraph in the history books. A classic cold warrior, he had defected to the West in '88. His reasons for doing so were deeply personal, and in a world defined by the opposing polar forces of avarice and ideology, his abrupt change in allegiance had been viewed with great distrust by the members of the intelligence community in his new homeland. Because he had not been a high-ranking member of a KGB directorate, but rather a field operator—someone used to doing the heavy lifting and the dirty work—his defection was not a coup. He would have served the cause better by remaining in the East, acting as a double-agent to be pushed around on their chessboard. Only Sir Charles had recognised his value, and at great personal cost, had given Konstantin Khavin his new life in the West, and more importantly, a purpose to go with it.

Despite his bluntness and sardonic, typically Russian, demeanour, Konstantin was a fiercely loyal and deeply honourable man. Sir Charles had earned his loyalty in a way that few would ever comprehend. The big Russian respected Frost for wanting to help Denison. It spoke volumes about the man in a language he could understand.

Frost was tagged for protection detail, but the question of *why* Denison had become a target was Konstantin's job to figure out. And the best place to start looking for answers was with the man himself.

Konstantin stood in the darkened interior of Denison's flat, giving himself a moment for his eyes to adjust. He'd seen part of the front room: tasteful, if masculine décor, lots of black and chrome, but very little to offer any unique personal insights beyond the fact he obviously lived alone. He heard the distinct ticking of a clock, smelled the aroma of...cinnamon? And then he caught a trace of something else. It wasn't subtle, but it still took him a moment to identify the cheap cologne that wasn't quite strong enough to mask the musk of body odour, and the sweet, faintly chemical smell of all-purpose gun oil.

Neither smell would have lingered long after the offending source had left, meaning he wasn't alone.

Konstantin tensed, hyper-alert to the rooms around him.

His entry hadn't been silent.

They knew he was here.

A handheld electric torch flared across the room, its beam picking out the sharp angles of the furniture before it speared towards him.

Adrenaline flooded through Konstantin, so that he felt cold and numb and paralyzed all at once. But he didn't hesitate. He threw himself forward and down, hitting the floor hard on his shoulder, and tucked into a tight roll. He came out of the roll close to the source of the light, but the move seemed to take an eternity.

He heard the unmistakable *whump* of a suppressed shot, followed instantaneously by the sound of the 9mm parabellum punching into the door. It would have opened a hole in his head if he hadn't thrown himself to the floor. The cone of light lanced through the dark apartment, chasing him, but Konstantin didn't stop moving. Not even for a second. He pushed up out of the crouch and lunged at the shadow where the gunshot had originated. The sulphur-smell of burnt gunpowder stung his nose. It was fitting that the room smelled of hell, because that was exactly where his would-be killer was going.

Konstantin barrelled into the gunman and took his legs clean out from under him.

He heard the muffled grunt as the breath punched out of the gunman as he slammed down on his back. He hit the polished hardwood floor *hard*, but before Konstantin could press home the advantage and finish the man off, pain exploded through the Russian's head. He took the blow on the temple. He threw up his left hand to ward off another blow, barely deflecting the second attacker's gun hand. The force of the impact shivered the length of his arm—but that was better than through the bones of his head.

It was life and death: the Russian's favourite stakes.

He gave his body over to violence, seeming to see each move and each blow a fraction of a second before they landed, meaning he could anticipate, act and react with punishing brutality. He blocked a desperate swing on his left arm, turning it aside and stepping into the retaliation, driving his elbow into the middle of his attacker's face. Bone and gristle crunched as the second man's nose ruptured and a shard of cheekbone drove back into his brain. There was no fight left in him after that.

Konstantin pulled his Glock from the holster beneath his left arm and pulled back on the slide. One in the chamber. He levelled the gun on the man on the floor and asked, "Who are you working for?"

The man looked up at him. He was on one elbow. His comrade lay dead on the floor beside him. He knew how this was going to play out.

Konstantin waited.

The man didn't say anything.

"You're not going to tell me are you?"

Nothing.

Konstantin squeezed down on the trigger. The gunman tried to throw himself out of the way, but only succeeded in moving the cause of death by about six inches as Konstantin's bullet tore open his throat.

It was messy.

And loud.

Konstantin stood stock still. The only sound in Denison's apartment was the harsh in-out rasp as he regulated his breathing.

So they'd sent two gunmen for Denison; that made things a bit more interesting. An attempted hit and run, gunmen in the park and assassins in his apartment. Whoever was after him, they had resources and manpower, doubling up on every job. That meant something.

Konstantin had killed both men—assassin and back-up—but that didn't mean there wasn't a third member of their team, and that realisation snapped him out of his inertia. He took up the discarded torch and with it located the fallen pistols—both were SIG Sauer P226 Tactical 9-mm semi-automatics, and both were equipped with suppressors.

He placed the torch alongside the barrel of his Glock and swept the room.

Nothing.

But he wasn't about to relax. That wasn't his way. He turned his attention back to the gunmen. A perfunctory search yielded a sheathed wrist-knife and a spare magazine for the SIG, along with a ring of keys, but no wallets or identification. In the first shooter's inside breast pocket, Khavin discovered an envelope, slightly crumpled and slick with arterial blood from the neck-wound. It was stiff, heavy, quality parchment. Denison's name was inscribed on the front: hand-written calligraphy, but with almost machine-like precision. The squared-off flap was open, but it had been sealed with an elaborate red wax seal. The remnants of the seal were imprinted with a familiar looking symbol.

He pocketed the envelope and turned his attention to the second gunman.

Khavin took out his phone, and with the torch shining on what was left of the man's face, captured his bland likeness digitally. The shattered nose wouldn't help the facial recognition software, but Lethe was good. He'd find a way to make it work. He took a shot of the other man, trying to get as little blood as possible in it. Then he put the earbud into his left ear and double-pressed on it, opening the line to Lethe in Nonesuch.

"I'm in," he said, not giving Lethe time to say anything. "Gate-crashed quite the party."

"You didn't get any blood on your suit, I hope?"

"I'm sending you a couple of pictures. There's not much of the guys left, but hopefully you can work your magic. I'll call when I have something more." He ended the call before Lethe could reply, and then forwarded the images to Nonesuch.

Still utilising only the torch, he moved from room to room. He was alone. He made a mental map of the flat, and then went through to Denison's study.

The study was sparsely decorated, a working space with a computer on the desk and several bookshelves lining the walls. He'd been expecting old-school money, leather-bound books, antique bookcases, leather-topped desk, but this room was very much in keeping with the black and chrome bachelor chic of the rest of the place. Konstantin took note of the titles of the books that lay on the desk: military strategy and tactics, current events. On the glass shelves above the desk there were a few trashy thrillers, and numerous copies of Denison's own published books. Did that mean Denison considered them on par with the trashy thrillers? Or was he reading too much into the room?

Konstantin took a seat at the desk and booted up the computer. He really didn't like the fact that the entire world was becoming so reliant upon computers, mainly because he really didn't like computers. Of course, it was password protected.

He called Lethe again.

"Jesus, Koni," the young man said, "I've only just got the photos into the facial recognition program. I'm good, but I'm not *that* good. Even I need half a minute. "

"I need you to get into Denison's computer. It's password protected."

"Ah, why didn't you just say so? Right. Plug your phone into the USB port, just like I showed you, and I'll take care of the rest."

"Already done." He switched the phone to speaker mode and set it on the desktop.

The advent of personal computers had completely changed the spy business. Instead of sneaking into a target's home, picking the lock on their file cabinet, photographing everything with a camera concealed in a cigarette pack, and hoping you survived long enough to get the film developed, or smuggling state secrets out on micro-dots, now it was all wireless. It wasn't even necessary to crack the password; Lethe could clone the hard drive and sort through the security protocols at his leisure back home in Nonesuch without getting his hands dirty.

Konstantin was old-school, though; there was value in the old fashioned approach. While Lethe droned on in the background, he took out the envelope he had taken from the dead gunman. There was no question that it had been Denison's, and given the fact the assassin had pocketed it, it was equally obvious that its contents were connected to the attempt on his life. Motive? Loose end? He opened the envelope and drew out a piece of crisp parchment, folded in thirds.

"Well that's a little…unexpected," Jude Lethe said suddenly. He blew out a sharp breath. "Okay. Got something on your party guests."

"Do tell." The Russian's reply was automatic. He wasn't paying attention. He was riveted by the document in his hands.

"The chap works for Universal Exports."

"And that should mean something to me?"

Lethe clucked. "I'm speaking metaphorically, Koni. I thought the KGB would have educated you on the popular culture of the United Kingdom. Universal Exports was something dreamed up by Ian Fleming. You do know about him, right?"

"James Bond."

"Very good. Bond's cover in both the books and the films was field agent for Universal Exports."

It took a moment for the implications to sink in.

A cover story.

Universal Exports was make-believe.

These guys worked for a make-believe organisation?

No. He'd connected the dots wrong.

"The guy with no face is Jim Benning. He works for the Royal and General Bank."

"And that's a cover?"

"Most definitely. But not any old cover. The bank is routinely used to establish cover for MI6 spooks. I would say I hope you haven't killed him, but I've seen the photos."

When Khavin did not reply for a moment, Lethe continued in a more urgent voice. "I need to tell Sir Charles about this, but...I think it may be Vauxhall that's after Denison."

Khavin read the brief handwritten message on the page again:

> *Tony, I cannot express the depth of my gratitude.*
> *Your search for the sword is truly a hero's quest... I*
> *daresay, a knight's quest. Your efforts will not be forgotten.*

The numbness returned. Two corpses. Both, almost certainly, spooks. He was in trouble. He needed to get out of there. He needed to get as far away from Denison's apartment as he could, as fast as he could, and he needed to warn Frost.

He picked up the phone, even though it was still in speaker mode, and held it to his ear. "I have got a lead here. I'm going to follow up. I'll be going dark."

"No, Koni." Lethe's voice was rock concert loud in his ear. "No leads, no rogue ops. You don't do *anything* until I get word from the old man."

"I'll be in touch," Khavin said, and clicked off.

He glanced at the paper once more before stuffing it into his pocket. It wasn't the message that filled him with equal parts dread and disbelief, but rather the distinctive crest rendered in full colour across the top of the page—the Crown and Castle of the House of Windsor—and the unfamiliar, but still very legible signature scrawled beneath.

MI6 was targeting a British subject for termination, and Konstantin had a pretty good idea of why. Proving it, however, would mean going places and doing things Sir Charles would most certainly not approve of.

So he was on his own.

FOUR
COMMAND AND CONTROL

Nonesuch Manor, Ashmoor—2020 UTC

"Thank you, Maxwell." Sir Charles folded his hands on his lap and gazed down the long gravel drive at the approaching limousine. The windows were tinted black. "If you'd be so kind as to wait inside." It was an order, not a request, no matter how politely it was couched.

The butler made a disapproving noise, but released the wheelchair's handgrips and turned on his heel to stride back inside the formidable manor house-cum-castle that was both the primary residence of Sir Charles Wyndham, and the headquarters of Ogmios.

Ogmios.

The old man had named the team after a Celtic deity—the god of eloquence and persuasion—who, oddly enough, was often portrayed as the Gallic equivalent of the Greek demigod

Herakles. Hercules. The comparison was no accident; the Celts rightly recognised strength as the most effective form of persuasion. But there was more to Ogmios than brute force. Ogmios the god was described as having chains that pierced his mouth—his smiling mouth—and tongue, and those chains extended to the ears of his followers. Sir Charles had always found this an intriguing notion; was persuasion, in the end, just another form of self-mortification?

And of course, Ogmios was supposed to stand against the herald, Mabus, and the Antichrist on judgment day.

It was fitting, if unconventional.

The team, of course, were no more straightforward than the god.

Persuasive strength, in the form of four very deadly operatives—Ronan Frost, Konstantin Khavin, Orla Nyrén, and Noah Larkin—guided by his own years of experience both in the field, before the Docklands Bombing, and in the diplomatic field since, and funded by a deep-black budget. They existed for one purpose: to defend the sovereignty of the realm. Not a terribly unique or original idea, but what set Ogmios apart from the other services was its manoeuvrability. Unfettered by bureaucracy, his team could react almost instantaneously to a threat. Any threat. The other side of that freedom was complete deniability. If anything went wrong, they could not claim the protections afforded to the official services; disavowal would be automatic, the cavalry would not charge in. There would be no rescue.

They were on their own out there, which suited Sir Charles just fine.

Set free from the hell of red tape and mandatory rimming of the Civil Service, Ogmios was in a position to actually accomplish some good in the world. Unfortunately, deep-black and deniable did not mean that his team were completely off-leash. Like its namesake, his team were chained, and the man that held the other end of the chain sat in the black limousine pulling to a stop in front of him.

Quentin Carruthers.

Onetime Vauxhall Cross spymaster, now Ogmios Control.

The team had only a vague understanding of this connection to Vauxhall. Both Sir Charles and Control intended to keep it that way. Face-to-face meetings were rare and usually conducted in a clandestine manner right out of the Cold War playbook. For Control to come to Nonesuch was unheard of.

Sir Charles considered what Lethe had just told him: two MI6 agents had been waiting in Denison's apartment, and Konstantin had killed them after being fired upon. If the Service were behind the attempts on Denison's life, the ramifications didn't bear thinking about. One conclusion was inescapable, though: Frost had no idea what he was facing.

Sir Charles had been mere seconds away from calling the Irishman in when the message from Control came in: "We need to talk."

The limousine's tyres crunched gravel as it pulled up beside the main portico. The driver got out and circled around to open the rear door for him. For a moment, the man stared blankly at Sir Charles, then seemed to grasp what the wheelchair actually meant, and smoothly recovered, offering a hand to assist with the transfer into the darkened vehicle.

The old man allowed himself to be drawn up out of the chair. His legs were useless so he was wholly dependent upon the driver to seat him. The man apologised as he rather gracelessly manhandled him into the back seat.

Control remained silent, cloaked in shadow, until the door was closed.

The driver remained there, standing with his back to the car. "You've really excelled yourself this time, dear boy. One might even say you've dipped your hand right into the beehive. Unfortunately, there's no honey in there, Charles."

Sir Charles regarded the other man. Effeminate. Pale. Dressed like a Victorian toff. He was the most dangerous man he'd ever met. "Get to the point, Quentin. We're not getting any younger."

Quentin Carruthers sighed. His reedy voice sounded like the air whistling from a balloon. "There was an unfortunate incident in Kensington Gardens tonight. I believe you are aware of it? Shots fired, general panic, that sort of thing. Of course, the official report will be some sort of crime spree. Something gang related, so we don't worry anyone unduly."

"I know you well enough to know you didn't come out here to make small talk, so how about I speed things up a bit? Ronan Frost was there. He took all the necessary measures to contain the situation. You know Frost, he's not a loose cannon. If there'd been any other way, he'd have taken it."

"As a matter of fact—"

"He was there to protect Anthony Denison from a hit squad. It was a personal request; they served together in Kosovo. But you already know all this, don't you? Those are my cards, laid out on the table. Now, tell me how Frost trying to save the life of a war hero has pissed in your cornflakes? Or do you want me to interpret it myself? I'm not sure you do. You see, you being here tells me that MI6 isn't terribly keen on keeping Denison alive. One might even go so far as to think that perhaps they're the ones who are trying to kill him. So, old boy, why don't you cut the crap and just tell me how Anthony Denison became an enemy of the Crown?"

Carruthers drummed the fingers of his right hand on his knee for a moment, seeming to think about what he was and wasn't prepared to say, and then leaned forward. "Have you ever heard of the Four Evangelists?"

Sir Charles sighed wearily. "Let's dispense with the give and take. Just lay it out for me."

For the first time, a hint of humour cracked Control's dour demeanour. "I always thought you rather liked the drama, my friend. Indulge an old queen for a moment: The Four Evangelists?"

"Something from the Bible; Book of Revelation, if I'm not mistaken."

"Human bodies, animal heads, messengers of God. Typical prophetic rubbish. They're also called 'the Four Living Creatures.'" He paused a moment. "Nothing else?"

Sir Charles shrugged. "Nothing comes to mind."

"Hmmm. Well, I'm not sure whether to be relieved or disappointed. It would seem this is one secret that Six has managed not to leak. The Four Evangelists are a secret society. Now, don't roll your eyes like that, Charles; such things really do exist outside the minds of conspiracy theorists. These aren't the usual suspects, though. Not the Freemasons or," and this time it was Control who rolled his eyes, "the Illuminati. They are an interesting mob, using the Book of Revelation as a blueprint for...well, no one's exactly sure what for. At least, not the minutiae. Disrupt the global status quo; that sort of thing."

"And I am to believe that Denison is a member of this group?"

"That's what Six believes. We don't go around murdering our own, Charles. You should know that. Six think that, whatever the Four Evangelists have planned, it's going to happen soon."

"You're lying, Quentin."

"I swear."

"Konstantin killed two of Six's men in Denison's apartment about thirty minutes ago."

Control rubbed at his face. When his hand came away, it looked as though it had lifted away the last layer of calm with it. "Okay. Okay. Yes. We outsourced the hit on Denison. A complete bollock job, and in no small part that is down to your men. Frost, and now Khavin. This isn't a game, Charles. I can't hold Six off. They've killed at least three of Her Majesty's men. You do realise what that means, don't you?"

"It means I have to look after my people." There was an accusatory note in Sir Charles' voice.

"It's all about damage control now." Carruthers shifted in his seat. "There's nothing for Ogmios here, Charles. Leave it alone."

"I have men in the field."

Control shook his head. "Frost is compromised. He's with Denison, now. You can't help him. Khavin, perhaps; but honestly, Six won't let either of them walk away from this. You have to let them sink."

"Like hell I do."

"You aren't listening to me, Charles. You don't have a choice. If you interfere with this operation, you're finished. Ogmios is finished. We're talking treason."

The old man bit back another retort even as it formed on his lips. It wasn't within Carruthers' authority to order him to do anything; that was the very essence of Ogmios' deniability. His role was merely to act as a conduit, supplying information about situations that were beyond the reach of the sanctioned government agencies, not to give them their marching orders.

Nevertheless, the threat was explicit. Ogmios could not escape the chains that defined its existence. Through clenched teeth, he said: "Are you finished?"

There was another uncomfortable pause. Carruthers shook his head. "No. You have to give up Frost. Six can use him to locate Denison and finish this. It ends tonight."

Sir Charles stared at him.

"You're asking me to sacrifice him? That's not going to happen. Not now. Not ever. Let me talk to Ronan; explain it to him. I'll have him bring Denison in. Everyone wins."

"It's too late for that. We can't trust that Frost won't put friendship ahead of duty. You should be grateful we're not demanding Khavin's head on a plate. You contact Frost; you'll only tip our hand." Carruthers shook his head again. "No interference. No warning calls. No negotiation. No contact whatsoever. You know how the game is played. A pawn sacrifice."

"Frost isn't a pawn. None of my people are."

"Charles..."

"Write this down, because I'll only say it once." He rattled off Frost's mobile number, not caring if the former spymaster was ready for it. "We both know that I won't throw him under the bus. I am going to do *everything* in my power to protect Frost. You need to tell your people that. Make sure they know that if they come after him, they are going to get hurt."

He reached for the door handle.

"There's nothing you can do for him, now," Carruthers persisted. "If you care about your people, about Ogmios, then you have to back away, Charles. This isn't a game. No tit-for-tat bargaining. Frost's a dead man walking."

"I doubt that very much, Quentin. But then, I've known Ronan a lot longer than you have, and I'd back him to take down anything that Six could throw at him. He's not some grunt." He pushed open the door.

Sir Charles said nothing as he struggled into the waiting wheelchair, but before he slammed the door on the conversation, he leaned his head back into the car. "After everything, you really don't understand what I've built here, do you? They stay with me because they know we are a team. We stand together. We fall together. You want to take one down, you have to take us all down."

He didn't wait for a reply, but brusquely slammed the door shut.

Refusing any further assistance, he wheeled the chair around and, fuelled by black anger, propelled himself across the portico to where Maxwell held the door open. Sir Charles didn't slow down. He pushed down on the wheels, keeping them spinning, intent on reaching the control room.

"Sir, please," Maxwell protested, four steps behind him. "Allow me."

Something about the manservant's tone—not his usual subtle sarcasm, but rather sincere concern—reached through the dark cloud, and Sir Charles drew up short, pulling back on the wheels and then raising his hands in surrender. Affecting his gruffest manner to spare them both a maudlin display of sentimentality, he growled: "Fine. Take me to Lethe. You won't believe what that bastard wants me to do. Well, I won't do it, Maxwell. Put on a pot of coffee. It's going to be a long night."

"Of course, sir. If you need *anything* don't hesitate, no matter what the hour."

"I appreciate that, Maxwell, but you're no good to anyone if you don't sleep."

"I could say the same, sir."

"You could, but I wouldn't listen."

By the time Maxwell rolled him into the Ogmios nerve centre, he felt he had the beginnings of a plan. It wasn't a good plan, but it was something, and right then, something was better than nothing.

Jude Lethe jumped up from his workstation, a guilty look on his earnest face, as if he'd been caught doing something indiscreet. "Sir..."

That wasn't a good sign.

Lethe was rarely formal and *never* at a loss for words.

"Go on."

"It's Konstantin. He's gone black. He said he was going to follow a lead."

Sir Charles nodded. "A lead. Good. That's what we need. Have you unlocked Denison's computer?"

"Only about thirty seconds after I cloned it. But that was the easy part. I haven't had a chance to go through his files yet to see if I can find anything useful."

"Look for any reference you can find to the Four Evangelists. And not just in Denison's computers; look everywhere. Start with MI6. Pass along whatever you find to Mr Khavin."

"He's not answering," Lethe repeated.

"Then put it somewhere he can find it when he needs to. Khavin knows what he's doing."

"And Frosty?"

Sir Charles pursed his lips. "Has he checked in?"

"Not yet. Should I call him?"

"No." He took a deep breath. "Make no attempt to contact him, Mr Lethe. In fact, I want you to block all calls from him. You can do that, can't you?"

Lethe's eyes grew narrowed. His lips pursed. "Block?"

"No questions, Mr Lethe."

"He'll think we've abandoned him, sir. He'll have no idea what's going on."

Sir Charles closed his eyes. No contact. Control had made that very clear. "Frost is on his own now. The sooner he realises that, the better, if he wants to see the sun rise."

"Shit."

"Very eloquently put, Mr Lethe. But yes. Shit."

FIVE
KNIGHT'S QUEST

London—2030 UTC

Frost picked out Denison and Lili loitering in the 'Arrivals' area, close to the Hertz desk. One thing about airports was that they were never empty. There was safety in numbers. They were also an infrastructure hub, with the best access to major rail and road networks. He pulled the rented Volkswagen Passat parallel to the curb right in front of them and flashed the lights, one, two, three times, to catch their eye.

Even though he had only rung off with Denison a few minutes earlier—a brief call directing him to this rendezvous—he felt a measure of relief at seeing them.

Parting company had been a strategic risk.

But every risk was exactly that—a risk.

He didn't think the men trying to kill Denison would be able to get ahead of them, but if by some chance they pulled off a hop-frog manoeuver, he'd gambled that the crowded Tube and the heightened security at the airport would offer a measure of protection if nothing else. But there were any number of ways things could have gone wrong. Not knowing who was behind the attempts on Denison's life didn't help. Different groups would have different thought patterns—and that meant different tactics. He needed to know who he was dealing with. It was as simple as that.

Denison climbed into the front passenger seat. Lili got into the back. Neither of them said a word as Frost pulled away from the kerbside pick-up point and back into the snake of traffic. Without indicating, he weaved between taxicabs and shuttle buses going to the Holiday Inn and Sheraton Skyline. Instead of turning into the lane that would lead them away from the airport complex towards the M25, he steered into one of the short-stay multi-storey car parks and accelerated up the ramp, changing up the gears as he pushed the VW faster and faster until they reached the open rooftop.

"Ronan?"

Frost ignored him, and yanked up on the handbrake, slewing the VW around tightly in a one-eighty to face back the way they'd just come. He killed the engine.

"What are you doing?" Lili barked from the back seat. Her accent was even stronger than before—and eerily familiar in Frost's ears. "We have to get to Saint Albans!"

"We're going nowhere until you tell me what's going on," Frost countered. There was no deference in his tone. "I can't protect you if I don't even know who we're fighting, Tony. It's as simple as that. No secrets. Not if you want me to help you."

Denison sank back wearily in his seat. A long, uncomfortable silence built between them before he finally met Frost's gaze. "Lili's right. Time is of the essence. I will tell you everything on the way, you have my word, but we *must* leave now."

For a moment, Frost almost yielded to the insistent plea. Old habits died the hardest. He gripped the steering wheel tightly and shook his head. "No." The word was no more than whisper. Simply saying it was enough to add steel to his resolve, though. "No, Tony. Not an inch until you answer two questions. Who is after you? And why?"

Lili muttered a harsh curse under her breath. He recognised the word immediately. It was Serbian. *What is he doing with...?* He jerked a thumb over one shoulder. "Why don't you start with her?"

Denison actually seemed to brighten at the suggestion. "Of course. Where are my manners? Ronan, this is Dr. Lilijana Pavic. Lili, Ronan."

Pavic? The name triggered a rush of memories. Before Ronan could act on any of them, Lili spoke. "Yes, we have already met, Mr Frost." Her voice was flat, but now the accent was all too familiar. "You came to our house in Pristina. I remember you: the young man with the old man's hair."

Frost glanced at Denison, who returned a knowing nod. "His daughter."

Frost craned his head around and gazed at Lili. He looked past the attractive, sharp-boned face and saw the truth of Denison's statement. This was, without a doubt, Kristijan Pavic's daughter.

He *had* met Lili before. She had only been a teenager at the time, and the meeting had been brief; a perfunctory handshake and nod of the head before getting down to business. Kristijan Pavic, a regional Serbian police chief, had politely introduced his family to the delegation from the task force sent to investigate reports of crimes against humanity in Kosovo—crimes committed by Serbs against ethnic Albanians.

Thousands had been slaughtered, entire villages wiped out.

Women and even young girls had been raped, not merely as an act of violence, but as a systematic effort to eradicate a race of people.

It was the very worst humanity had to offer.

The international response, sluggish as such things always were, had arrived too late for many of the victims. But once some semblance of order had been restored, the task of identifying and prosecuting the ringleaders had begun. That was why Ronan was there. Kristijan Pavic, despite his Serbian heritage, had cooperated unhesitatingly in the effort to bring the monsters to justice. It wasn't just some sense of national guilt. , a humanist, sick at the suffering of innocent people, and the first to come forward to help erase the collective stain of guilt that tainted all Serbs in the eyes of the world.

It had been a laborious, bottom-up process, modelled on the aftermath of the Holocaust. The men who had physically carried out the atrocities were connected by the chain of command to military officers and government officials, and while some of the latter believed themselves beyond the reach of prosecutors, including even Slobodan Milošević, the former President of Yugoslavia, men like Ronan Frost were there to make sure they weren't.

Although public awareness of the pogrom faded with the passage of time, replaced by newer and more immediate tragedies, the investigation had continued relentlessly, reaching out like tendrils of ivy, insinuating into the concrete wall of silence that had for more than a decade protected the men ultimately responsible for the campaign of ethnic cleansing.

Frost had followed the news of the investigation, at least insofar as he was able to, given the diminishing level of media coverage, and had recognised the names of several of the accused men. The majority were local officials, men he had dealt with personally during *Operation Agricola*, and who had at the time seemed to offer full cooperation with NATO forces and international observers.

Men he had trusted.

That had taught him a valuable lesson about humanity.

Even so, Frost had been surprised by the news that Kristijan Pavic would be the next Serb brought before the World Court at The Hague to answer for crimes against humanity.

But that hadn't been the end of the matter.

Pavic's trial, which was still underway, hadn't gone according to script.

The case laid out by the prosecution consisted mainly of hearsay: the testimony of men who stood to gain in some way by Pavic's downfall. News pundits had begun openly calling the proceedings 'a witch hunt' and many believed that if Pavic was not completely exonerated, the credibility of the international court must be called into question.

Frost reserved judgment.

Appearances could be very deceptive.

Sometimes, you had to trust the universe to sort itself out, and that had been, he thought, his final position on the matter of Kristijan Pavic.

So what was the man's daughter doing in the back seat of his car, accompanying Tony Denison, the pair of them running for their lives?

Frost turned back to his former commander. "Okay, that's a start. Now what this is about? Pavic's trial?"

Denison shook his head. Frost saw a hint of his earlier reticence returning. So much for cards on the table. "Nothing to do with that at all. But in terms of getting you into this mess, yes, that's down to Lili, but only because when things got ugly, I immediately thought of you." His gaze wandered for a moment. "Ronan, have you read my books?"

The question caught Frost by surprise, but before he could answer, Denison pushed forward. "Okay, it doesn't matter if you haven't, I won't take it personally. I'm not after a review. But if you have read them, then what I'm going to tell you might not sound quite so daft."

"I'm not much of a reader."

Denison nodded. "Okay, but I am sure you are familiar with my position on globalization. It's an abomination. Multinational corporations have effectively taken over the world. They have completely corrupted the democratic process, using money and influence to put their cronies in positions of power—I'm not just talking about the backwater countries of the developing world, it's happening right here. Cultural identity is being wiped out. These corporations have completely legitimised their dominance by stripping away the local laws that might have held them in check. The New World Order has emasculated and enslaved us all."

Frost realised he was holding his breath.

Despite Denison's warning, the abruptness with which he launched into what amounted to a paranoid diatribe struck Frost as odd. It wasn't him—or at least it wasn't the man he'd served with. If it had been anyone else, he'd have offered him a tinfoil hat. "And it's this New World Order that's after you?" he asked, carefully. He spoke slowly, in an effort to conceal his scorn. "Because you're trying to expose them in your books?"

"Oh, dear Lord, no, nothing like that." He actually smiled, which relieved Frost. Perhaps he wasn't suffering from paranoid delusions after all? "Those with the intelligence to see what's going on already know, the rest of the Great Unwashed are so addicted to consumerism, they don't see the chains of their own slavery. No, Ronan, they're not afraid of what I might say."

"So what are they afraid of?"

"What I'm *doing*."

"And what is that?"

Denison glanced at Lili, who nodded, then looked back at Frost. "The greatest threat to the New World Order is nationalism. Sovereign nations, defending their borders, imposing tariffs, putting the needs of their subjects ahead of the desires of the corporations—these are the single greatest obstacles to the institution of one world government. As I said, the democratic process has been corrupted. Are you familiar with the old saying: 'In a democracy, people get the government they deserve'? People are inherently selfish, so it's a simple thing to appeal to their self-interest at the polls. What good is a government of the people when the majority of the people are too selfish, or just too plain ignorant, to see past their desire for immediate gratification?"

Frost narrowed his eyes. "You want my vote?" He said. He avoided political discussions like the plague. He'd grown up in a world defined by ideological conflict—*violent* conflict—and knew from experience that the most seductive arguments were often the most wrongheaded. Like the song said, meet the new boss, he's just like the old boss. Very little ever really changed. "Like it or not, Tony, that's the way it is. We're a democracy."

A gleam appeared in Denison's eye. "That's where you're wrong, my boy. We are, and have always been, a monarchy...the *United Kingdom*... the *British Empire*. We are not a democracy."

"Tony, that's ancient history and we both know it."

"No, it isn't." Denison's tone had suddenly become clipped. It was obvious he'd taken offense to Frost's off-hand dismissal.

"We have strayed from the path, to be sure, but we can still find our way back."

Frost pondered this statement and the pieces at last began to fall into place. "So that's your game? Restore the monarchy? Convince the Queen to take back the reins and dissolve Parliament? That'd get rid of the latest bunch of inmates running the asylum, I suppose. And this New World Order? They're so worried that you might succeed they're willing to kill to stop you?"

"Ronan, they've tried. You saw it yourself."

Frost couldn't argue that. He wanted to though. He wanted to say that Denison had gone off the deep-end.

"I freely admit that my ambition is to put the monarchy back in charge. Not the Queen, though, as she is too old now to rule, and Charles is weak, tainted by his treatment of Diana—William is the answer. He is fundamental in restoring faith in the Crown. He is loved like his mother was. That's what I mean to do, and that's what the New World Order is trying to prevent."

Every time Denison used that phrase, it sent a shiver of apprehension down Frost's spine. When he had taken the call—scarcely more than an hour ago—his reaction had been automatic: when your mate's in trouble, you drop everything and help. But this? New World Order conspiracy nonsense? A bid to restore the monarchy? This wasn't him. He'd served his country for most of his adult life, unreservedly and without question. He wasn't a Royalist though, or even fiercely patriotic. He was a modern day warrior.

And yet, someone *had* tried to kill Denison.

That was one unassailable truth.

Bullets didn't lie.

So, if not agents of some mythical New World Order, then who?

And why?

He needed to know more.

"Explain it to me again, Tony. And remember, I'm just a simple Irishman. Speak slowly and use small words."

There was the faintest hint of smile, but then Denison's face hardened resolutely. "I will, but only if you start this car and put us on the road to Saint Albans. Deal?"

It was like a hostage negotiation—you had to give something to get what you wanted, and Frost wanted the truth. Whether or not Denison gave him a straight answer, his decision was already made. In answering his old mate's call, he'd made a tacit commitment to see this through to the end. It didn't matter if he was bat-shit crazy. He was in trouble, and short of outright treason, he would do whatever it took to protect his friend.

With a defeated sigh, he started the car and pulled out of the parking slot, only half-listening as Denison resumed speaking.

SIX
SWORDS AND STONES

2042 UTC

Frost couldn't decide if Denison sounded slightly less mad, or more mad, as he repeated his conspiracy theory, augmenting the discourse with inflammatory—and almost certainly unverifiable—vignettes about the operations of the New World Order and its primary constituent, the mysterious Bilderberg Group.

It occurred to Frost, as he steered the VW onto the M25—the original Highway to Hell—that he hadn't heard from Lethe. That was unlike the guy. *Maybe he couldn't climb the New World Order's wall of secrecy?* He thought mordantly. Still, he couldn't ignore the single, unarguable fact: someone had tried to kill Denison.

He double-tapped his earbud, but Nonesuch didn't answer.

He killed the call and resolved to check in as soon as they reached Saint Albans.

Speaking of which... "Okay, mate, let's say I accept all this," Frost said, cutting Denison short. "What's so important about Saint bloody Albans?"

The glare of oncoming headlights briefly illuminated Denison's face, revealing a wide, almost boyishly eager grin. "That is where we will find what we need to establish the absolute and supreme authority of the Crown."

Frost thought the comment sounded rehearsed. It was obviously meant to sound portentous. Instead it sounded manic. "And exactly what would that be? The Holy Grail?"

"Don't be facetious, Ronan. There's no such thing. No; in Saint Albans we will find the Sword," Denison said reverently. "Remember your legends: 'Whoso Pulleth Out the Sword of the Stone and Anvil, is Rightwise King Born of All England.' Do you know that quote?"

"King Arthur. I had the right story." Frost felt another straw settling onto the camel's back, ready to break it. "You aren't seriously trying to tell me that Excalibur is waiting for us in Saint Albans? Please. Don't do this to me, Tony."

"The sword in the stone was called Caliburn. Centuries of telling the tale have confused the two. And of course, some exaggerations have coloured the accounts. But make no mistake: the sword is real. It was once the symbol of a king's right to rule. And I believe it can be again."

Frost thought about pulling the car over and kicking the pair of them out on the hard shoulder. He felt like he'd stumbled into a Monty Python film. He shook his head. "This is a treasure hunt?"

"It is *the* treasure hunt, old chap," Denison replied with that same, wild intensity. "The sword is *the* symbol of Britain. But don't be fooled by children's stories: there's nothing inherently magical about it. It is just a sword. In the hands of the rightful king, though, it will send a powerful, resonant message to all Crown subjects. Rule Britannia. We've all wanted that for so long. Why do you think everyone still adores the royals? It's not some misguided loyalty to the past. It is in our blood. We're all just waiting for them to stand up, like something out of Arthurian legend: the Once and Future King will guide us out of the wilderness."

Michael Palin's voice echoed in Frost's head: You can't expect to wield supreme executive authority just because some watery tart threw a sword at you.

He took a moment, making a show of checking the mirrors as he tried to temper his disbelief. "And this sword is real? Arthur, Merlin, the Round Table, Camelot...all that was real?"

Before Denison could reply, Lili broke her long silence. "No, no. Tony is being metaphorical. There was no Arthur, so how could we be looking for his sword? We are talking about the Crocea Mors; the sword of Julius Caesar, last wielded by the *Dux Britanniarum*."

Frost looked at Lili through the mirror. He was still unclear on why Denison was in the company of Kristijan Pavic's daughter, but he recalled how Denison had introduced her: Dr. Lilijana Pavic. He guessed she wasn't a physician.

Denison offered a guilty shrug. "Lili is the expert. She should probably explain it."

"Expert?"

"PhD in Classical History from Sapienza. She knows what she's talking about."

Lili didn't wait for further prompting. "Pay attention, Irishman, because I will not talk slowly or use small words. There is no mention of a 'magic sword' in Julius Caesar's extensive account of his campaign in Gaul. This is not surprising, since the Romans abhorred superstition. It is only in the *Historia Regum Britanniae*, the History of the Kings of Britain, written by Geoffrey of Monmouth some twelve hundred years later, that we read of Caesar's battle with Prince Nennius. As Nennius and Caesar fought, Nennius sustained a head wound, but the sword became lodged in Nennius' shield. The prince took the weapon and continued fighting with it, and every man he faced was mortally wounded. The sword, which allegedly shone in the sunlight, was believed by the Britons to possess supernatural powers. Geoffrey called it 'Crocea Mors,' which means 'Yellow Death' in Latin. And, as was their custom, when Nennius died from his wound a few days later, he was buried with the blade. According to Geoffrey, he was entombed in the North Gate of London.

"But Geoffrey's account is a romance, not a history. His sources were oral traditions and legends, handed down from one generation to the next, and no doubt influenced by the eventual occupation of Britain by the Romans and countless other invading forces. Caesar himself made no mention of the battle, or of Prince Nennius, much less the loss of the sword. By itself, that is not surprising; like any victorious king, Caesar's ego would not have permitted him to record such a defeat. However, I recently discovered a palimpsest that cast new light on this chapter of history."

"Palimpsest?"

"A palimpsest is a document written upon a previously used piece of parchment. Vellum was expensive, so it was not uncommon in times past to scrape the ink from a scroll and reuse it. With modern X-ray technology, it is sometimes possible to recover the original document. Several months ago, a document that had at one time been in the private collection of Benito Mussolini, was discovered to be just such a palimpsest. The original document, at least what could be recovered of it, was a letter believed to have been in the possession of Octavian, Julius Caesar's successor, who took the name Augustus Caesar when he became the first emperor of Rome.

"In the letter, Titus Labienus, a former tribune and one time ally of Julius Caesar, makes reference to the battle with Nennius and the loss of the sword. He furthermore identifies it as 'the Sword of Mars' taken by Julius Caesar from the Temple of Jupiter. Labienus offers to journey to Britain and recover the sword from the tomb of Nennius. He claims that possessing the sword would symbolise Octavian's right to rule in Caesar's stead; a sort of divine stamp of approval."

"Sounds familiar," Frost muttered. "So, the Roman version of Arthur's story?"

"Such themes are common in legends. The sentiment, however, is distinctly…" she paused thoughtfully. "*Unusual* for a Roman."

"Did Octavian take him up on his offer?"

"It is impossible to say, and frankly irrelevant."

"Irrelevant?"

"The palimpsest offers independent verification that the sword exists, and that it was buried in Nennius' tomb."

Frost checked the mirrors again, using the moment to digest what he had just been told. He was no student of history—or legend—and there was nothing particularly appealing about the thought of running down a fairy tale about a magic sword. It was hard to reconcile his memories of his former commander, a pragmatic and disciplined man, with the man in the seat beside him.

"So, Caesar's sword then," he said finally. "Sorry, but why would discovering an old sword shake the foundations of society? It's not like you're saying Jesus had a daughter."

Denison didn't wait for Lili to weigh in. "Geoffrey of Monmouth tells how a later king, Vortigern, in the fifth century, removed the sword from Nennius' tomb, had it hammered into a crack in an anvil, and set atop a great stone in the town square of London as a war-memorial. The sword, anvil, stone and all, was later moved to Silchester, where Arthur was able to draw it forth, thus signifying his right to rule all England. So you see, it is both Caesar's and 'Arthur's' sword."

Frost rubbed at his temple. He adjusted the mirror so that it was angled toward Lili's face.

"There is reason to believe that Vortigern was an historic figure, and we now have evidence that both Nennius and the Crocea Mors really existed." Lili drew a breath. "However, there are some problems with accepting Geoffrey's record as entirely factual. According to his account, Nennius was buried in London's North Gate. But in the time of Nennius, London would have been nothing more than a small tribal settlement. Nennius' tribe, the Catuvellauni, occupied a stronghold in the ancient city of Verulamium, just north of London in modern Hertfordshire—"

"Where Saint Albans is today," Frost said.

"I told you he was quick," Denison said, casting a knowing glance over his shoulder.

"If Geoffrey got that detail wrong," Lili continued, "then the account of what Vortigern did is suspect. It may be that there was a sword in an anvil, but it would not have been the Crocea Mors."

Frost wondered if that distinction would really make any difference among those inclined to accept that an old war relic constituted divine approval; but maybe that was the whole point. Denison didn't linger on that detail. "Arthurian lore is something of a passion, and I am intimately familiar with *Historia Regum Britanniae*. When I learned that there was evidence indicating that Nennius was a real historic figure, I got in touch with Lili—"

There was a subtle change in Denison's voice and Frost sensed there was a lot more to their relationship than the man was letting on.

Another complication he didn't need right now.

"—and then…well, let's just say I was able to enlist a very influential patron who shares my passion for history and legend. It has been well established that Saint Albans was the site of a major Iron Age settlement predating even the Roman city of Verulamium. Trying to narrow down the location of Nennius tomb, however, is more problematic. What if the Romans built their city on top of it?"

Lili answered the rhetorical question. "The ancient Britons would have buried their honoured dead in a sacred place: caves in a hill, for example, away from their settlement. When the Romans built their city, they would have used the existing settlement as a foundation. We know from the historical account that in the early fourth century, a Christian resident of Verulamium—Albans—was martyred on a hill outside the city. According to folklore, his severed head rolled down the hill and a well sprang up where it came to rest. The hill upon which he was martyred is now the site of the Abbey Church and Cathedral of Saint Albans. But it is the hill itself—Holywell Hill—that is of interest to us."

"With the help of my patron," Denison said, "we were able to arrange for a ground-penetrating geophys survey of those sites, and yesterday our efforts paid off. The survey team reported finding an extensive network of voids—tunnels—running underneath Holywell Hill; possibly even under the Abbey Church itself."

"Underground? At the risk of raining on your parade, we're not exactly kitted up for an excavation."

"I had all the equipment we were going to need in my car," Denison sighed. "But the survey shows several spots where the tunnels are very close to the surface. If we choose the right spot, we should be able to break through in short order."

"Break through? With our bare hands? In the middle of the night? Tony, is any of this even legal?"

There was a long pause, and in the dim glow cast by the dashboard lights, Frost could see the conflict in Denison's expression. To his surprise, however, it was Lili who answered. "Have you understood nothing? It is urgent that we find the Crocea Mors. Our enemies have already found us. We cannot delay. Not even an hour."

Denison slowly exhaled, then spoke with a more subdued tone. "Although he cannot officially sanction our search, my patron has given us tacit permission to do whatever we must; but it is critical that we act as quickly as possible. The surveyors will soon make their findings public, and once that happens, our adversaries will be able to hide the sword away for good. They won't be put off by questions of legality; they make the laws, after all. However, once we find the sword and put it in the right hands, the question of whether we've committed a misdemeanour or two will be moot. We're not looking to steal the sword and sell it on the black market. We only want to put it in the hands of its rightful owner. Trust me, Ronan; you're on the side of the angels."

Frost sighed, gripping the leather contours of the steering wheel, and wondered again, what had he gotten himself into?

A buried treasure—a magic sword, no less—hidden in a secret passage under an old church; it sounded ridiculous.

Tony and Lili could worry about breaking the secret codes and solving the riddles; his job was just to keep them alive.

SEVEN
TOMB

Saint Albans—2104 UTC

The Cathedral of Saint Albans and the orchard green below didn't look like the sort of place you'd go digging for a two-thousand-year-old relic.

Frost said as much as he gazed up at the dimly-lit structure atop Holywell Hill.

"Most of what you can see from the outside was built or renovated from the nineteenth century on," Lili explained patiently. She'd lied: she was obviously prepared to speak to him like he was an idiot. "But even the earliest Christian buildings antedate the battle between Caesar and Nennius by more than six hundred years, so don't expect to find clues in the architecture."

That wasn't really what Frost had meant.

He'd not visited Saint Albans before, but he had grown up in the shadow of Saint Columb's Cathedral in Derry, and that had coloured his expectations.

Though he hadn't been back home in ages, he vividly recalled the severe spire of Saint Col's stabbing into the heavens; it could be seen from almost anywhere in the county. Saint Albans was a little more *subdued*.

Although it did have the distinction of being the longest cathedral in England, its elegance and grandeur were a little more down to earth.

And unlike the dark Gothic austerity of St. Col's, the long but relatively low nave of St. Albans was formed of light-coloured stone and ringed in Romanesque flying buttresses that appeared to serve an ornamental, rather than structural purpose.

Somehow, it just didn't look *mysterious* enough to hide a treasure out of legend.

They'd parked the car just off Abbey Mill Lane, near England's oldest surviving public house: *Ye Olde Fighting Cocks*. It would be a good place to fall back to, Frost decided, once the night's adventure was done. Even treasure hunters needed to sleep. Either they could celebrate the successful recovery of the Crocea Mors or they could drown their sorrows in a pint of bitter.

Denison produced a sheaf of papers from a coat pocket and began studying them in the glow of a small keychain-sized LED torch.

After a few seconds, he looked up to orient himself with the geophys map and then gestured to a stand of trees on the south-eastern boundary of the orchard green. "That's our best bet," he announced. "The tunnel is less than a meter below the surface, and we can use the trees for cover."

Frost let out a sigh. "Forgive me for belabouring this point, but we still don't have anything to dig with."

"A tyre iron ought to do the trick. There should be one in the boot."

Frost tossed the keys to Denison. "Be my guest. I'll go see if I can't scrounge up something better."

He turned and headed up the hill, setting a brisk pace. He really didn't want to talk anymore. He wasn't sure how much more bullshit he could swallow.

Denison's presence felt like a black hole, sucking common sense out of the air. Now he had finally broken free, or at least, put some distance between himself and the man, he felt *normal*. But the only way to truly break free would be to tell his old mate to piss off—and that wasn't on the cards. Not while people were still shooting at him. No matter how stupid the reason felt. That didn't mean he had to buy into Denison's crazy quest.

Rock, welcome to the hard place, *he thought*.

What he really needed was a different perspective; an outsider's opinion.

He slipped his Bluetooth earbud in again and double-tapped for Lethe back at Nonesuch. Instead of the expected electronic trill, he heard three distinct and familiar tones, followed by a recorded operator's voice informing him that his call could not be completed.

The earbud was a satellite uplink; it wasn't reliant on the mobile network. It didn't go out of range or drop out just because he'd wandered off the beaten track.

He double-tapped again.

"Your call cannot be completed at this time."

He didn't like it.

He didn't like it at all.

He left the earbud in as he climbed the hill.

The cathedral grounds were empty, but Frost stayed in the shadows as much as possible. He skirted the exterior of the vast structure, and on the north side, tucked into the shadows cast where the nave met the transept, he found what he was looking for: a shed filled with grounds-keeping equipment.

There was a padlock on the door latch, but it wasn't really designed to keep anyone out. Inside, amidst a variety of electrical and petrol-fired mowers, hedge-clippers and chainsaws, Frost found two spades and a mattock, which he hefted onto one shoulder. He also acquired a folded tarpaulin and a beat-up old handheld torch that he carried in his free hand.

He returned to find Denison and Lili crouched over a patch of grass.

Denison was using the end of the tyre iron to outline a rough square where he intended to begin his excavation.

Frost handed one of the spades to him, and without comment, commenced carefully scraping up the turf. He rolled it back in a single unbroken section like a surgeon peeling away skin to expose what lay beneath.

The first half-metre of dirt yielded quickly to their shovels and they piled it on the tarpaulin, but beneath that, they hit a layer of hard clay that wasn't so easy. Several blows from the pick end of the mattock cracked the clay and loosened the earth, but digging down through it left both men filthy, blistered and exhausted.

Denison grinned triumphantly as the head of the mattock sank deep into the ground.

"I think we've found it," he announced.

With caution tempering his growing enthusiasm, Denison worked the spot for several minutes until he'd opened a hole through which loosened soil began to disappear like water down a drain. Denison shone his light into the opening. "We're close," he said, directing his words to Lili, who, despite her earlier, dour manner, now seemed to be holding her breath, caught up in the madness of the moment.

Frost cautiously moved to the edge of the waist-deep pit and began chipping at the thin layer of limestone to widen the opening.

Denison dropped to a prone position beside the hole and shone the beam of his small torch into the darkness.

Frost couldn't tell if he saw anything, but when the breach was large enough, his old friend turned and began lowering himself into it. A few moments later, he was peering up from inside the void.

"This is it," he declared. "There's evidence of digging and old wooden support beams."

Without waiting for an invitation, Lili clambered into the hole as well.

Left with no choice, Frost followed suit.

He switched on the torch he'd liberated from the groundskeeper's shed, but even in concert with Denison's keychain light, the darkness was overpowering.

An intaglio of reddish-black chisel marks marred the white chalk walls, and in the dim light, they looked to Frost like a malevolent curse inscribed in runes. He played the light back and forth trying to establish a mental map of the passage, and found the rough-hewn wooden struts Denison had described. The old timber crumbled to dust when he probed it with a fingertip.

"Ah, Tony, I'm not so sure this is such a good idea. The whole thing could come down with a sneeze. It's only held together by a wing and a prayer." When his friend did not answer, Frost directed his light ahead and found that he'd been left behind. "Bollocks."

They had entered in the middle of a tunnel that sloped up to the right and down to the left. He followed the glimmer of Denison's light as it reflected off the roof of the passage to the right and caught up to the others just as they paused to inspect a two metre-deep niche in the left hand wall. Over the dark curve of Lili's shoulder, he saw an amorphous mound that, upon closer inspection, turned out to be a human skeleton.

When it had been interred, the remains had probably been adorned in armour of wood, leather and iron, but time had left little intact. Yet, there was no denying that this was a purposeful burial, and the discovery of it, right where Denison had said it would be, was at least one point in Denison's favour.

"It isn't Nennius," Lili declared.

Frost was surprised by just how swiftly she'd reached her conclusion. "How can you tell? Is there a headstone or memorial I'm not seeing?"

She shook her head. "The Catuvellauni had no written language. And even if they did, they would not have recorded the names of the dead."

"Okay, then how are we supposed to know the right pile of bones when we find it?"

"Do you see this sword?" She helped herself to Frost's torch and played the beam along the resting figure's torso. Frost didn't see anything that he would have identified as a sword, but there was a long, rust-encrusted smear that appeared to have fused with the skeletal fingers holding it. "It has a leaf-shaped iron blade," she explained. "The hilt is decorated with carved pieces of bone. Nennius was buried with the Crocea Mors, which is almost certainly a Noric steel *gladius*. Very distinctive. Shorter than this Celtic sword, with no cross-guard."

"That should narrow it down," Frost muttered, not caring if she caught his sarcasm. He backed away as she came out of the niche.

They resumed their exploration of the main passage.

The funerary niche proved to be the first of several that lined both sides of the tunnel.

By some unspoken mutual agreement, Denison began searching the tombs on the right side, while Lili took the left. Frost dedicated his efforts to making sure no one came up on them unannounced.

He was surprised at the amount of effort the ancient Catuvellauni tribe had put into shoring up the necropolis. When Denison had described a network of tunnels underneath Holywell Hill, he'd imagined natural caverns created by water eroding random fissures in the limestone. The ancient Britons hadn't been content to simply stuff their dead into whatever cracks they could find, though. They had excavated the tunnels to an almost uniform height, just fewer than two metres, and laid down oak planks to form a continuous floor. They'd braced the ceiling every few metres with upright support pillars. It was obviously a proper work of engineering, even if the wood had long since rotted away. Frost had no difficulty imagining the barrow as it had been two thousand years earlier, with a procession of mourners carrying a fallen king to his final resting place.

It was humbling.

He shone his light into one of the recesses and illuminated the skeleton therein. As before, the grave goods had succumbed to rot and corrosion. Perhaps Lili had the expertise to identify the artefacts, but Frost saw nothing remotely recognisable as, well, anything. He moved on, inspecting two more tombs that were, while not exactly identical to the first, uniformly nondescript. Then, in the fourth niche, his torchlight fell on something that stopped him in his tracks.

"I think I've found something," he called. His voice echoed much more loudly than he'd intended. When Lili arrived at his side a few seconds later, he pointed his light at the object that had caught his eye. "That's Roman, isn't it?"

Lili was silent for a moment, but Frost saw that she was shaking her head slowly. "No," she whispered. "No, no... This is wrong."

"What do you mean?"

"This shouldn't be here," she said.

Denison crowded in behind them and added his torchlight to the tableau while Lili's hoarse denials continued. Frost looked again, wondering what he'd gotten wrong.

The niche contained a posed human skeleton, adorned with the same shapeless mass of decomposed clothing and armour that had fused to the other bones, but with a significant addition: directly in front of the bier, affixed to the end of a spear that protruded from the tunnel floor, was a human skull, still wearing a half-dome shaped cap of metal. At the base of the shaft, scattered among a pile of disconnected bones, was a jumble of metal plates.

He was no expert, but he'd seen enough pictures of Roman soldiers at school to recognise pieces of *lorica hamata* armour. The armour was standard issue for a Roman soldier of the first century BCE. Unlike the iron weapons and armour of the Britons, the bronze and steel used by the Roman legion was in markedly better condition.

So why was Lili on the verge of tears?

"They would not have done this," she said, still shaking her head in disbelief. "They would not have defiled the sacred place of their ancestors with the remains of an enemy."

Frost was beginning to understand: it was about honour.

Soldiers hadn't changed that much in two thousand years, it seemed.

Denison placed a hand on Frost's shoulder and spoke in a low voice. "The ancient Celtic tribes believed that the burial was a gateway to the afterlife. A rite of passage. Burying an enemy in the same tomb as your king would be tantamount to sending that enemy to join him in heaven."

"It makes no sense," Lili said.

Frost stared at the deliberately placed puzzle of bones. "They ripped him limb from limb and put his head on a pike. You don't have to be an expert to read that message."

Lili looked up sharply. "Really? And what do you read here, then? Tell me."

"'Keep out.'" Frost said. "My guess, they caught this guy trying to break into the tomb and decided to make an example of him."

Even in the dim light, Frost could not help but notice the abrupt change that came over Lili's face. "My God..."

She stared at the skull for a moment, and then dropped to her knees and began rifling through the heap of bones and metal.

Frost glanced at Denison, but his old friend appeared equally confused by her actions. "Lili?"

She didn't look up. "He tried to rob the tomb, but was caught and killed. His body left as a warning. It's the only thing that makes sense. And who do we know that wanted something from Nennius' tomb?"

There was silence for a moment, and then Denison said: "Labienus?"

"The answer was right there in the palimpsest. Labienus was asking for permission to go and retrieve the sword." She shook her head disparagingly. "We were foolish to assume that was the end of it."

"And this is Labienus?" Frost asked, pointing at the skull. "Or what's left of him?"

"Or one of his cohort..." Lili's voice trailed off as she found something in the pile of bones. When she withdrew her hand, she was delicately holding a long tube that might have been made of bronze or leather—it was so decayed Frost couldn't tell which. With painstaking care she began picking at it with a fingernail. Despite her cautious touch, huge sections of the tube broke away as soon as she touched them.

"Shouldn't you be doing that in a laboratory?" Frost asked.

"There's no time." Lili's voice was whisper quiet, urgent, as if she was afraid a single breath might cause her discovery to disintegrate completely in her hands. "There is a scroll in here. A message from two thousand years ago. It may tell us where the Romans were taking the sword."

There was an eager gleam in Denison's eyes, and for a moment, Frost felt it, too: the discovery wasn't just a clue that would bring them one step closer to their goal, it was proof that they were on the right track. It was proof of a legend even he'd grown up with. He understood now how a normally rational and cautious man could be completely seduced by the lure of buried treasure.

And then Frost saw something that made him forget all about dead legionaries and magic swords.

It was subtle—a faint change in the level of ambient light and a gentle shift in the angle of shadows cast on the wall of the main passage—and anywhere else he would have dismissed it or missed it entirely.

Several metres underground however, when the only sources of light were a nearly spent torch, a keychain light and the screen of Frost's mobile phone, all three focused into the burial niche, it meant one thing and one thing only: "Someone's coming," he said, keeping his voice low.

Lili did not look up from her labours, but Denison did. He turned to gaze down the tunnel. "They've found us!" He said, louder than Frost would have liked.

Frost had a pet theory: the denial response was an evolutionary trait. It was the result of many generations of hominids playing dead to avoid being eaten by stalking lions on the African savannah. And despite years of training and experience, which had honed his reflexes and his instincts, his first impulse was still go for the obvious denial—there were any number of possible explanations that didn't involve secret societies and conspiracies. They'd dug a hole in a relatively public place, and there was no telling who might have stumbled across it: a curious local out for his evening constitutional; a drunk on his way home from the pub; the cathedral groundskeeper looking for his stolen tools; even one of the local plod, following up on a call about people digging on the green. Maybe this once, it didn't have to be the worst case scenario? That inner voice that had kept him alive for so long laughed at him. A cold tingle of adrenaline pulsed through him, and without consciously thinking about it, he drew the Browning.

He put a finger to his lips, and then edged forward, peeking out of the niche and peering down the length of the passage.

He saw two spots of light floating in the darkness. Definitely advancing.

First job: determine intent. He wasn't going to let them get any closer before he knew what kind of threat they posed.

He flashed his light in their direction.

The response was immediate.

A section of the passage no more than a metre from where he hid puffed out a spray of stone chips and dust. A moment later, the sound like sledgehammer blows filled the tunnel.

Well, that answers that, Frost thought, pulling back another precious inch, trying to disappear into the wall.

He reached around the corner with the Browning and pumped two quick shots in the direction of the lights. He wasn't trying to hit anything. He just wanted them hesitant. The pistol's report filled the niche. Lili clapped hands over her ears. Denison didn't so much as flinch.

More silenced rounds split the air, these ones striking stone and old wood. A third volley shot harmlessly past the niche to impact somewhere in the darkness beyond. They traded shots for nearly a full minute, until the air was thick with dust and cordite.

Frost pumped another pair of shots down the narrow tunnel.

Through the ringing in his ears, he heard a muffled grunt and a sharp cry of pain, but before he could press home the advantage, the niche dissolved into a miasma of smoke, dust and noise as another sustained volley of shots tore into the fabric of the tunnel around them. He tried to read the chaos: best estimate, four men, and given the ferocity of the sustained fire, they were nowhere near exhausting their ammo.

Frost had two full thirteen-round spare clips along with five left in the Browning. They wouldn't last forever, even with restraint.

"Of course!" Lili's voice nearly made him turn. He couldn't worry about her if he wanted to stay alive. She was carefully examining the contents of the scroll case. She'd managed to unroll the brittle parchment, keeping it more or less intact. Cracked and faded, the script was still legible. "How could

I have been so stupid?" Lili berated herself, oblivious to the danger they faced.

"What does it say?" Denison pressed.

Frost didn't care what it said, unless it contained a failsafe get-out-of-jail-free card, this being the jail.

There was a lull in the incoming fire. It didn't make things any better. The tunnel was still choked with dust and fumes. He tried to listen for anything: a tell-tale crunch of a footstep, whatever would betray the gunmen's advance.

Frost wasn't a victim. And he wasn't about to become one.

He grasped Denison's shoulder. "Use that survey to find us a route out of here."

"There is no way out. We had to dig our way in. The entrance has been buried for two thousand years."

"I don't care. Find another spot close to the surface. We dug our way in; we'll dig our way out, if we have to. Just be ready to move when I give the signal."

He didn't wait for an answer. Frost aimed into the heart of the dust cloud and burned through the rest of the magazine, grouping the bullets two to the left, one in the centre, two to the right. Even before the report of Frost's last round subsided, the clay walls exploded as a storm of lead tore up the passage.

Frost slammed a fresh magazine into the Hi-Power, but held back.

Denison and Lili were urgently studying the survey, tracing paths through the maze of tombs. "Get ready," he repeated. "As soon as there's a break in fire, we're out of here. Understood?"

The only reply was a terse nod from Denison; Lili didn't even glance up.

After thirty seconds, the tumult ceased with unexpected abruptness.

Frost waited for the lull to pass.

It always did.

He counted out eleven in his head, and then barked: "*Go!*"

Denison took Lili by the hand and sprinted headlong into the dark.

Frost watched them go.

Then followed.

He had only gone four steps when a hollow metallic *clang* clattered on the tunnel floor. He didn't need to see it to know exactly what it was.

There wasn't time to shout a warning, and any shout would have lost reaction time, anyway. Frost sprinted full pelt forward, arms thrown wide, and tackled the others like a prop forward and drove them to the ground an instant before the grenade detonated.

EIGHT
THE FOUR BEASTS

Nonesuch Manor—2056 UTC

Sir Charles sighed and rubbed the bridge of his nose, trying to fend off a persistent headache.

He looked again at the information displayed on the monitor.

"Feast or famine," he said, and glanced over at Lethe. Surrounded by keyboards and monitors, with a row of empty energy drink cans lined up along the edge of his desk, the young man looked strangely helpless; all that information at his fingertips, and no way to put it to use.

"Enough," Sir Charles declared. "Mr Lethe, what do we *really* know?"

The young man blinked at him. "Sir?"

"It's a question of facts. We have all the information we need. You could argue we have too much. Now it's time to make sense of it. And that means going outside of our comfort zones. Let's join the dots."

Lethe nodded slowly, his unspoken reply: *I'm the tech guy. I dig. I exploit flaws in systems and open back doors. I'm not an analyst.* And it was true. When it came to collating raw data Lethe was a wizard, but parsing the data was a different thing. It took a different mind-set to put what he found in a human context. Therein lay the double-edged sword of progress.

Sir Charles possessed a lifetime of experience—he'd played and survived the game of Cold War era espionage. He was a strategist. A schemer. He lived in a world where intuition rather than information determined the moves and countermoves. It was one such an 'intuitive leap' on the part of MI6 that had led to the order to terminate Tony Denison. He knew that. No doubt they thought it was regrettable that Frost was caught up in the process, but when it came right down to it, he was an acceptable loss. Collateral damage.

The old man needed to find a way to get ahead of the game.

Intuition or information? It was a false choice. One without the other was useless.

"Like Alice, we need to start at the beginning. So only the facts: what do we really know about the Four Evangelists?"

Lethe started rattling out a rapid sequence of taps on his keyboard, but Sir Charles raised his hand. "Forget the Internet, Mr Lethe. I said what do *we* know. We've already read everything Google has to offer on the subject, so synthesize it for me."

Lethe stopped typing, but his fingers didn't stop moving. He made a fist with his right hand, and then unclenched it, spreading his fingers wide. He was uncomfortable, but the old man didn't care. Comfort wasn't a luxury any of them had.

"Think of it as a pop quiz."

"That doesn't help. The name comes from the Book of Revelations—"

"*Revelation.* Singular. Common mistake."

Lethe blinked. "Is that important?"

"I have no idea, but it is a fact. Do go on."

"Well... according to Six, this group believes that *Revelation* isn't a religious vision at all, but a blueprint for world domination." Lethe drummed his fingers on the desk, obviously itching to back up his words by calling something up on the screen. "The seed of the idea was first put forth by an Italian historian—Lorenzo Martedi—who postulated the idea that John of Patmos wasn't really a Christian at all, but a sort of guerrilla leader, trying to organize a revolt against Rome. Evidently, someone caught onto the notion of using the same plan in a more modern setting, though there's only anecdotal support for the existence of the group."

"Anecdotal?"

"Rumours circulated from Internet chat rooms; conspiracy theories and such."

"And Vauxhall takes these seriously?"

Lethe shrugged. "That's the thing about conspiracy theories. If enough people start talking about them, they have a way of becoming real."

"And what particular theory do the Four Evangelists espouse?"

"Nothing particularly new. One of the dominant themes in conspiracy circles has always been the emergence of one world government. It's the great slumbering evil; the forces of Mordor and the Galactic Empire all rolled into one. One theory goes that global agencies—the United Nations, the World Bank, and so forth—were prophesised in Revelations... Revelation...as dragons and monsters trying to take over the world. The Four Evangelists think they are on the side of the angels, opposing the rise of the Antichrist."

"And I would assume Brigadier Anthony Denison been linked to this conspiracy because of his vocal opposition to globalisation. Is there a more explicit connection?"

"I don't know." Lethe's hands went for the keyboard, but he stopped himself. "For what it's worth, I found stacks of conspiracy-related nonsense on Denison's hard-drive, but no explicit mention of this particular group."

Sir Charles rubbed the space between his eyes again, trying to focus his mind. He was bone-weary, but rest wasn't a luxury any of them had. Not if they wanted to help Frost. "Does Six name any other likely members?"

"Quite a few, actually. Anyone who's ever overtly expressed pro-nationalist sentiments is on the watch list; it's rather like a witch hunt."

"I take it that 'Four Evangelists' isn't meant to be a literal assessment of the group's numbers. You said the group has a secular interpretation of the book of Revelation. I believe you used the word 'blueprint.'"

"That seems to be Six's position. The faithful don't take it upon themselves to fulfil the prophecy; they sit back and wait for God to make it happen."

"That's assuming they don't believe that God has chosen them to be agents of the Divine Will." Sir Charles shook his head. "A blueprint? How so?"

Lethe's fingers finally stopped twitching, and Sir Charles realised that he had asked the right question. "A picture's worth a thousand words," Lethe said. He rattled out a command line and a moment later, the array of wall monitors filled with lines of text.

Sir Charles began reading it aloud: "'And round about the throne, *were* four beasts full of eyes before and behind. And the first beast *was* like a lion, and the second beast like a calf, and the third beast had a face as a man, and the fourth beast *was* like a flying eagle. And the four beasts had each of them six wings about *him*; and *they were* full of eyes within: and they rest not day and night, saying, Holy, holy, holy, Lord God Almighty, which was, and is, and is to come.'"

"The 'beasts' are the Four Evangelists," Lethe said.

Sir Charles kept reading. "'And I saw in the right hand of him that sat on the throne a book written within and on the backside, sealed with seven seals.' I think we've found our blueprint, Mr Lethe."

NINE
WHITE HORSE

Westminster—2118 UTC

Konstantin Khavin strode confidently up the walkway. He felt the growing intensity of the gaze of the uniformed constable who stood between himself and his ultimate goal: the main entrance to Clarendon House, one of several official residences for members of the Royal Family located in the City of Westminster. When he was within five metres, the man spoke in a polite but authoritative voice: "Closed to the public for the day, sir. Sorry. You'll have to come 'round tomorrow if you want the tour."

Konstantin's didn't break his stride. He raised one hand and let the flap of a black leather wallet fall open on the gold badge of a Metropolitan Police Inspector, along with an identification card bearing his picture. Both were near-perfect forgeries capable of withstanding any visual scrutiny. They'd also pass most electronic methods of verification. Konstantin had lived in England long enough to mask the worst of his

Russian accent with concentration. "Inspector Kennedy, Counter-terrorism Command. I need to speak with the watch commander. Now."

The other man bristled a little. It was always a territorial pissing contest. He wasn't going to let someone from the Yard just walk up and order him around without making him work for it. He dutifully examined Konstantin's fake ID, and then keyed his wireless headset. "There's a man from CTC here, sir. Says he needs to speak with you."

The man's gaze was no less suspicious, but after a moment he nodded. "Chief Inspector Baxter has the watch tonight, sir. He's in the security office…you know the way?"

"Nope. I've never been inside before," Konstantin said, wondering if the seemingly innocent question was the shibboleth that would expose him as a fraud. The fact that the constable immediately delivered a rapid fire set of directions and then stood aside to admit him, did not entirely allay his concerns.

Once inside, Konstantin ignored the constable's detailed directions and began roaming the halls of the manor house.

The doors to a number of ground floor rooms stood open, no doubt part of the public tour, and Konstantin passed these by without so much as a second look. He wasn't interested in what they had to say about life, the universe or anything else. He was more interested in the closed-circuit video cameras that watched from the ceiling at regular intervals. They were discreet, but if you knew what you were looking for, easy enough to spot. The place was quiet. He only saw a few members of the household staff, and they were busy with their duties. There were no other officers from the Protection Service inside that he saw. After a few minutes of wandering unescorted, another constable caught up, halfway up a flight of stairs he wasn't supposed to be climbing.

"Inspector Kennedy?"

Konstantin noted the use of his alias. It was safe to assume someone from the security team had been following his movements on the CCTV and they'd exchanged radio reports with the guy on the door. He turned to the uniformed officer, feigning embarrassment. "Sorry. This place is a maze."

A polite nod was the only acknowledgement. "If you'll follow me, sir."

Konstantin turned and followed him back down the stairs, falling into step behind the constable. The man led him turn after turn, through double sets of fire doors, on an unerring path to a part of the first floor that clearly wasn't on the tour. The policeman knocked on an unmarked metal door and then, without waiting for a response, turned the knob and pushed it open.

No key card or numeric security pad, the Russian noted. Very typically British. Trusting. Old-School.

The office, like the door, was a strictly utilitarian affair. Functional. In other words: *ugly*. Instead of priceless *objects d'art*, the walls were adorned with dry-wipe boards and tacked-up bits of paper with things like rosters, circuit duty and the day's visitors on. Konstantin noted the bank of flat screen video monitors that displayed static images of the hallways. The central screen showed a graphic representation of the floor plan, but before he could get a good look at it, the room's lone occupant rose from behind an MDF desk and addressed him.

"Kennedy, is it?"

Chief Inspector Baxter appeared too young to have a senior position in Protection Services, but Konstantin suspected that wasn't a liability at all. He had the straight back and bearing of a military man. Along with his athletic physique and chiselled features, he might have stepped right out of a recruitment poster.

Konstantin took a deep breath; the lie would need to be smooth.

"Inspector James Kennedy, Counter-terrorism Command. I apologize for showing up unannounced like this, but I've learned of a credible threat to His Royal Highness."

Baxter's expression was unreadable. He said nothing, but motioned for Khavin to take a chair. Only when both men were seated did the watch commander break his silence. "Well, let's have it." There was a hint of sarcasm in Baxter's voice, but Konstantin couldn't quite tell if it was directed at the message or the messenger.

"There's a new group. Radical nationalists. They call themselves 'The Four Evangelists.'" Konstantin's pause was unintentional; although he'd read and reread Lethe's email, which had told him precious little about the group Tony Denison was allegedly affiliated with, it was the first time he'd spoken the name aloud, and it felt awkward on his tongue. If he'd been naming a terror cell, it would have been a much more brutal sounding name: something stark and threatening. The Four Evangelists just sounded wrong in his ears. "We've received a tip that they are planning to make a move against His Royal Highness."

"The Four Evangelists? Sounds like the name of a gospel music quartet."

"Even so, all indications are that the action is imminent."

Konstantin recalled the salient points of the email, the fruits of Lethe's hasty search of the secure MI6 database, the far-flung fringes of the Internet, and his sub-ether network of contacts. "The name is taken from the Bible; the Book of Revelation."

Baxter waved a dismissive hand. "I don't care where the name comes from. Just tell me what they're planning, and what you think I should do about it."

"The prince is vulnerable here." *Understatement of the year*, Konstantin thought. When he'd grasped the significance of the letter he'd found in Denison's flat, and determined his next course of action, a quick trawl of Internet newsgroups dedicated to following the everyday activities of the royal family had given him the exact location of the man who had written the letter. The royal family provided constant fodder for professional journalists, amateur paparazzi, and obsessed fans alike. Despite the fact they had around-the-clock security—provided by the elite Protection Command of the Metropolitan Police—those resources could only stretch so far. There were always going to be points of vulnerability. It hadn't taken the Russian long to identify one that might well be exploited—at least by him, to prove his point.

"He should be moved to a secure location." The Russian paused a beat before adding, "I'd like a chance to brief His Royal Highness on the situation."

"Perhaps you'd like to ask for an autograph while you're at it? Sit for a photo?"

Konstantin's leathery face creased, but before he could protest, Baxter laid his hands flat on the desktop and leaned forward. "I came over to SO14 from CTC just six months ago. Funny thing, Inspector Kennedy, I don't recall *ever* seeing you before. But we must know some of the same people." The Chief Inspector let the comment—both an accusation and a challenge—hang in the air between them.

Konstantin let his mask of outrage slip.

Baxter had called his bluff. Any protest would only make what he was about to do that much harder. His spread his hands guiltily. "Seems I chose the wrong cover."

Baxter likewise abandoned all pretence of civility and professional courtesy. He stood abruptly, one hand dropping to the butt of the pistol holstered on his belt.

"Before this gets nasty, let me explain." Konstantin leaned back in his chair and quickly raised his hands in a show they were empty. "It's true; I'm not with the Yard."

"Tell me something I don't know?"

"I work for the Crown. I'm with Special Branch, and if you know people there as well, I'd be happy to compare names, birthdays, favourite colours and bad habits."

Baxter held his aggressive stance but made no move. "First it's CTC, now SIS. Why should I believe you?"

"Six is foreign affairs. It's out of my hands. I've kicked it up the chain. Eventually bureaucracy will catch up, and the message will get to where it needs to go, but there's no time for that." Khavin lowered his hands. "Look, I apologize for the deception, but believe me; *everything* I've told you is legit. I can show you."

"You do talk a lot of shit, don't you?"

Khavin slowly reached for the breast pocket of his jacket, and as he did, Baxter bristled.

"I'm going for my mobile," Konstantin explained, moving slowly. He held the lapel of the coat open to show that he wasn't concealing a weapon. With even more exaggerated slowness, he dipped two fingers into the pocket and brought out his smartphone. He tapped the screen a few times, bringing up the email message Lethe had sent, and then placed the device on the desktop. "It's all there. Read it for yourself."

Baxter kept his right hand on his firearm, but warily reached out for the phone with his left. He had to lean forward slightly to reach it from his standing position, and when he did, Konstantin made his move.

He struck with the swiftness of a viper.

He seized Baxter's wrist and yanked the man toward him, twisting the police supervisor around so that his back slammed down across the desktop. Konstantin wrapped his left arm around Baxter's throat and squeezed the sides of the man's neck between his forearm and biceps. At the same time, he clamped a firm right hand over the policeman's own, holding both the hand and the gun immobile.

Khavin could feel Baxter's raw strength—the man was no seven-stone weakling—as the policeman struggled against his chokehold. It didn't matter how strong he was. Konstantin had him on his back, and he couldn't get any kind of leverage, meaning he couldn't offer any sort of counterattack.

"I don't want to hurt you. Nod if you understand?"

The policeman's eyes were wide. Angry. He understood plenty. So did Konstantin.

Baxter's movements became more purposeful.

He tried to wriggle a hand in between his throat and Konstantin's arm.

The Russian closed his vice-like grip even tighter.

"Don't make me do this," Konstantin said flatly, but Baxter wasn't giving up the struggle. He was frantic now. Panicked.

Thirty seconds.

Baxter's hand fell away from his throat.

He began frantically tapping the Russian's forearm. It was urgent. Almost polite.

The security cop had almost certainly been trained in ground fighting techniques—grappling, jiu jitsu and the like—but it was one thing to learn them and another to use them to fight for your life. Konstantin was a fighter. But more than anything else, he was a survivor. The impulse to tap out had been a desperate, instinctive reaction; a primal part of his brain, programmed by hours of mock combat in a gymnasium, had taken over. Safety signals carried no weight in the real world.

Konstantin maintained the pressure until Baxter's struggles weakened and finally ceased—and then just as quickly he released his captive and made sure he was still breathing. He used Baxter's own handcuffs to bind him in his chair. Two of Her Majesty's government employees dead, one unconscious in fewer than two hours. He wasn't exactly making friends. And it was going to get worse. Much worse.

Konstantin scooped up his phone and helped himself to Baxter's radio. He emptied out his gun and pocketed the shells. The whiteboard on the wall opposite the desk detailed the duty stations for the night watch. The protection detail comprised of four men, not including Baxter; two in stationary positions near key exits, and two on roving patrol. The Russian studied the CCTV monitors, looking for the patrol.

Next, he turned his eyes to the central screen with the manor's floor plan.

In a room on the second floor, just below a label that read "Office #3," there was a black bar with a six-digit designation code. It was a radio frequency; the Royal Protection service had put an RFID tag on their charge. Konstantin watched the monitors for a few seconds longer, ensuring that his route was clear, and then left the office at a brisk walk.

Less than a minute later, he was standing in the doorway of Office #3, staring at Tony Denison's secret patron.

He was older than Khavin expected—the camera obviously added as many years as it did pounds. It occurred to the Russian that they were probably of an age. He had never been one to follow the royals, but he recalled a time when the prince's personal life had been the stuff of tabloids and scandals almost daily. That kind of 'news' had played well in the Soviet Union; it was a tailor-made example of bourgeois excesses in the West. But even then, a mere foot soldier in the Cold War, Konstantin had taken such propaganda with more than just the metaphorical grain of salt. Still, it was the image of the prince that had stuck in his head: a young man in polo kit, carousing with models and actresses, frittering away the wealth stolen from the working class. *We both got old*, he thought, looking at the man.

The prince was seated behind an elegant antique desk, pecking away at a computer keyboard. A two-finger typist. He glanced up as the big Russian entered, and then his gaze locked on the Glock in the intruder's hand.

"I have no wish to harm you, Highness." Khavin now made no effort to conceal his accent. "But if it happens..." He gave a little shrug. "I won't shed a tear."

To his credit, the prince remained calm. "What can I do for you?"

The question threw Konstantin. It was polite. Cultured. He'd been expecting a demand to get out. A threat in return. He had been so caught up in the audacity of what he was attempting that he hadn't really thought through exactly what he hoped to accomplish if he pulled it off. And suddenly, here he was, face-to-face with the prince. There were questions that needed answering, suspicions that needed to be confirmed, and both were made all the more urgent by the brief postscript Lethe had attached to the briefing on the

Four Evangelists. Konstantin had felt an ominous chill as he'd read the words: *"Frost has been cut loose. The Old Man says that whatever it is you're doing, do it, do it well, and bring Frosty in from the cold."*

Ronan Frost was not exactly his friend. He didn't have friends. But they were a team, even if in name only. They were a collection of lone wolves working towards a common goal.

And yet he felt a kinship with Frost and the others that was so much more profound than something as simple as friendship.

The idea that one of his brothers-in-blood had been set adrift made his soul ache.

There was nothing he wouldn't do to help Frost.

Likewise, roles reversed, the Irishman would move heaven and earth to help him.

If that meant throwing away his career, his freedom, perhaps even his life, he would do it.

It was that simple.

So here he was.

Now what?

There was no time for indecision. Elaborate deception would have given them time to regroup. *The truth then...at least, just enough to set the hook.*

He strode briskly across the room, keeping the Glock trained on the prince, and tossed the folded letter onto the desk. "You wrote this, yes? Tony Denison does this for you?"

The prince's eyes dropped to stare at the parchment.

His silence was all the confirmation Konstantin needed.

"The sword?" he pressed. "What makes it so important?"

The prince looked at him, weighing him up. It was hard to tell from his expression whether he found Konstantin wanting. "The Brigadier is doing me a personal favour." The prince looked up slowly from the letter, meeting the Russian's gaze. "I can't imagine why this would be of interest to your government."

He thinks I'm FSB. Khavin suppressed a smile. *Good.* Sir Charles may have given his blessing, but there was no way the old man would have authorised shaking down one of Her Majesty's family, no matter how many steps they were removed from the throne. And even though Khavin had made it clear that he was acting without orders when the shit hit the fan, it would be all over Nonesuch. So, if the prince wanted to believe he was a foreign intelligence agent, well, it wouldn't hurt. "I am the one asking the questions," he said sharply, exaggerating his accent to almost cartoonish proportions.

"Very well. The sword is an historical artefact. If you know anything about me, then you know that I've a keen interest in archaeology."

"Let's assume I don't share your interest. So, tell me, is it worth a lot of money?"

"Money?" The prince seemed appalled by so crass a suggestion. "I would imagine it's priceless."

"But that's not why you want it, is it?"

Silence.

"Denison was the target of an assassination attempt tonight," Khavin continued. "Several, actually. Does that surprise you?"

"Someone tried to kill Tony? Is he—?"

"Still alive."

The prince slumped in his chair. "Who? Who's behind it? Who would do such a thing?"

Once more, Konstantin debated what tack to take, and decided again that the truth would yield the best results, and the quickest. He forced a guttural laugh. "You don't know?

These would-be assassins work for your own government. British Intelligence, Your Highness."

A look of horror crossed the royal's face. "Impossible. You're lying."

Now, Khavin thought. "They believe they are protecting *you*. You see, they think Denison is one of the Four Evangelists."

"Tony isn't..." The prince caught himself. A blank mask slipped easily over his face; this was a man used to lying. "I don't have the slightest idea what you are talking about, I'm afraid. You should go now. While you still can."

From the moment he'd read the prince's letter, Konstantin had known exactly why MI6 had elected to sanction the hit on the former brigadier, and Lethe's email had only served to confirm his theory. The search for a relic was irrelevant; a smoke screen. What mattered—and the only thing that mattered—was that an outspoken critic of British foreign policy, a man believed to be part of a radical nationalist conspiracy, was doing an off-the-books favour for the Crown. That fact would be beyond embarrassing if it ever got out. Add to that, Six believed the conspirators were gearing up to launch their offensive.

And right up until that moment, the only question Konstantin had had was whether the prince had been included in the decision to terminate Denison.

Now he had his answer.

'Tony isn't...what? Isn't one of the Four? And how could Your Highness know that?

The squawk of radio noise sounded in his ear: "*Base, this is North Gate. Radio check, over.*"

He glanced at his wristwatch. 21:29. The sentries were a minute early with their scheduled call-ins.

When Baxter didn't respond, someone would come to investigate. It would take no more than two minutes before someone discovered what he had done.

But he couldn't go now. Not without knowing more.

"I think you know *exactly* what that means. The Four Evangelists...who are they? *What* are they?"

The prince stared back, no sign of inner turmoil.

He really was a very good liar.

So Konstantin threw subtlety to the wind.

"Denison will be killed, and you'll never have your sword. My..." he leaned heavily on the desk as he said, "*employers* don't know whether that is a good thing. They are concerned about variables which might destabilise a delicate situation. They said to me: 'Go find out which side of this we want to be on.' So you tell me: why is the sword so important?" He rested his knuckles on the prince's antique desk, and leaned in. "Are you one of the Four Evangelists?"

The other man slowly deflated back into his chair. "I take it you don't really know anything about them."

Lethe's message had described them as some kind of quasi-religious conspiracy with Biblical leanings, but without the proper context, it was difficult to grasp exactly what he meant. What, precisely, was the difference between one religious indoctrination and another? The Bible held no more significance to him than the Quran, the Bhagavad Gita or for that matter any lunacy like Dianetics. They were all just make-believe. The only truth he knew for sure was that regardless of what any of those books actually said, extremists would find a bloody and violent way of interpreting Holy Writ.

The prince didn't wait for a reply. "I was a fool to have gotten mixed up in this. David made it sound so innocent...so perfect."

"David?" Konstantin said.

"David Habersham. An old acquaintance."

Konstantin noted the shift in tone and diplomatic choice of words. The prince was already looking for ways to distance himself from the situation. "And Habersham is one of the Four?"

The prince appeared not to have heard the question. "The Book of Revelation describes four angels, each with the head of a different animal. Traditionally, they have been associated with the authors of the four gospels, and so are often called 'the Four Evangelists.' In Revelation, the four bear witness to the opening of a scroll with seven seals. When each seal is broken in turn, something...well, something fantastic occurs."

There was another hiss in Konstantin's ear. "Base, it's North Gate. Do you copy?"

The prince misread the slight shift in the Russian's expression. "You don't know *any* of this, do you?"

"I may have missed a few days of Sunday School."

"When the first seal is broken, a white horse rides forth. According to the prophecy, the rider of that horse wears a crown."

The mention of the horse triggered something in his memory. "The Four Horseman of the Apocalypse?"

"Ah, so you do know *something* about it."

"What does this have to do with Habersham?"

"David is, as you have already surmised, part of this group. But they aren't what you may think; they're not radicals or extremists at all, and they're certainly not religious ideologues trying to make the prophecies come true."

Konstantin already understood that much. Lethe's message had been colourful as ever: *Using Revelation as a blueprint for some nefarious scheme.*

"Habersham believes that Revelation was never intended to be a book of prophecy. Rather, it was a coded message. A way of disseminating a strategy designed to break the hegemony of Rome."

"Rome? As in, the Vatican?"

"The seven parts of the scroll were seven steps to the plan, and the first, most important part was the establishment of a legitimate ruler who would be able to lead the cause." The prince managed a rather guilty smile. "A unique interpretation, to be sure; but, if you'll humour me a moment, the idea is not entirely without merit. We know very little about John of Patmos. For years, it was believed that he was St. John the Divine, but many scholars have come to believe he was a different man altogether. He may even have been a political exile, intent on co-opting Christianity as a foundation for his revolt."

Konstantin checked his watch again. The prince was talking, but he wasn't talking fast enough. Not about anything important. He clenched his fist. He needed to go. But he wasn't about to. Not while the pieces were beginning to fall into place. There wasn't a clear picture, but he felt certain that he was on the verge of...well, a revelation. "The rider of the white horse wears a crown. Is that what Habersham promised you? A crown?"

That odd smile tugged up the corners of the prince's mouth. "Oh, believe me; I gave up any such ambition a long time ago. The crown is not for me."

The crown....

The United Kingdom was a monarchy in name only. The crown was a symbol, an echo. It belonged to a lost era; the House of Windsor was nothing more than a celebrity family. But as long as the framework for the Empire remained intact, there was always the possibility of a return to the former glory. If the right person wore the crown.

"Not for *you* perhaps," Konstantin said as another of the pieces fell into place. "But perhaps you want something more for the next king. With the crown, he could be more than just a figurehead." He was sure he was missing something. "What I don't understand is where Habersham comes in? And the sword?"

The prince shook his head. Just once. Dismissively. "Symbolism. The sword is an historic symbol of royal authority. News of its discovery would generate a great deal of positive publicity for the crown, and if that came at the right moment... well, David understands this. He's the one who first brought to light Tony's quest to find it. It's all perfectly innocent, though. I can't believe lives are in danger because of this. It's not like we're talking gunpowder, treason and plot."

Konstantin wondered if Habersham felt the same way.

The Four Evangelists weren't just a social club. They weren't trying to curry favour with a highly placed celebrity for his endorsement. They weren't goofy or well-meaning or simply bat-shit crazy; whatever they were planning was dangerous and real and serious enough for Six to loose the hounds.

But where did that leave Denison?

"Base, are you there? Al?" There was an undercurrent of concern in the voice; the two minutes were up. They'd found Baxter in the control room. There were still too many unanswered questions, but he was out of time.

"Where's Habersham now?"

A look of concern crept over the prince's face. "Why?"

Konstantin felt a rush of frustration; the prince was stalling. He wanted to reach across the desk, grab the man by his jug ears and pound his head off the desk. But he didn't need to; sometimes the threat of violence was all a man needed. He'd let the Glock drift down, but with a snarl, he brought it back up and thrust the muzzle at the man across the desk. "Where is he?"

The prince blanched. "On the continent. The Netherlands, I think."

Konstantin nodded. He lowered the gun and backed to the door. "Some advice. Next time, Highness, choose better friends."

And with that, Konstantin pushed open the door and ran.

TEN
THE WRONG SIDE

Saint Albans—2132 UTC

Frost felt like he'd been fired from a cannon.

The detonation hammered through his body, punching him off his feet as it drove a spike of sheer blinding black agony through his skull. Sight, sound, smell: they all became one as his senses overloaded. He couldn't see anything. He had no way of knowing if his eyes were open or shut. Tinnitus rang in his ears, agonizing and intense.

He couldn't feel the ground against his body. His arms and legs refused to move.

Awareness returned in desperate gulps as he heaved down mouthfuls of choked air like a drowning man. But no matter how much he struggled, he couldn't get his head above water.

I'm alive.

It was one thought. One sentence. Two words. But it meant everything.

It wouldn't stay that way if he didn't move, though.

"Tony!" He couldn't hear himself speak. His mouth was full of dry chalk dust. His nasal membranes stung with the residue of explosives. "Lili!"

Denison's voice reached him. "We're all right."

A faint glow appeared less than a metre away; Denison's keychain torch, its tiny pinpoint of light shredded by the settling cloud of dust.

"What happened?" The voice was Lili's. Her words were faintly slurred.

Frost blinked through the pain in his skull. "They bailed back up to the surface and tossed a grenade down behind them. We got lucky. It rolled back down the tunnel before it blew. Otherwise we'd have been out for the count. The tunnel focused the blast."

"Fools," Lili spat. "They could have collapsed the tunnel."

"I think that was the idea." As if to underscore his supposition, a deep vibration groaned through the rock beneath him. "We've got to get out of here."

Frost struggled to his feet. He patted himself down, checking for injuries. His fingers found several tender spots, but no open wounds. He'd live.

Denison moved close enough that Frost could actually see his face in the glow of LED, but everything else remained fogged by the settling dust. "I can't find the survey map," he said. "I don't know which way to go."

"Well let's just start by getting the hell away from here." Frost knelt, and after a few seconds of fumbling around in the rubble, found his Browning. He pulled his mobile phone back out of his pocket, and added its glow to Denison's light.

The tunnel groaned again.

This time, he felt something the size and weight of a hailstone glance off his shoulder. Debris, some larger than his fists put together, rained down behind them. The aftershocks. The grenade had undermined the structural integrity of the barrow. It was caving in.

"We have to move," he repeated.

Frost took charge. He spread his arms out, as if to gather the others under his wings, and began moving them up the passage, as quickly as they dared in the dark. Frost had lived with one genuine fear all of his life: being buried alive. He felt his skin going clammy. His heartbeat quickened. He tried not to think about the weight of earth pressing down on his head. He just wanted to get out of there. Fear was the enemy.

He pushed them on.

They rounded a bend in the tunnel, and after a few more metres, the air began to clear. Their lights revealed the extent of the blast damage.

A standard M67 fragmentation grenade with 200 grams of high explosives was more than enough to ruin anyone's day, especially when coupled with a deadly spray of steel shrapnel driven at ballistic velocities by the blast. But while the passage had shielded them from the worst effects of the grenade, the unique geology of the warren—riddled with natural and man-made void spaces—had transmitted the shock wave like the hollow body of a kettledrum. And as the ground under Holywell Hill shuddered around the initial blast, some of those cracks had widened, and pieces of stone that had sat, unmovable, for centuries, began to shift like the grains of sand in an hourglass.

They hurried passed more funerary niches, barely noticing the shadowy pockmarks in their haste. Several had collapsed, and were spilling bones and rubble into the passage.

Frost had expected the after-effects of the blast to diminish the further they moved away from the immediate blast zone, but even two more curves on, well out of the immediate damage radius, the state of the ruin verged on catastrophic.

As if reading his mind, Lili said: "The passage is a spiral. We are circling around again and again, moving above the place where the grenade detonated."

"We're going up?" Frost hadn't noticed that, but in the unfamiliar and cramped environs of the tunnel, made all the more chaotic by slabs of fallen stone partially blocking the way and canted at bizarre angles, it was impossible to stay oriented, unless you were a walking GPS.

No one replied to the question, but as they continued along the tunnel, the truth of Lili's observation became apparent. The grinding groans of shifting rock and collapsing timbers increased, and then ebbed as their course brought them around again and again, higher up the hill.

As they approached another rubble-strewn section of passage, Lili disappeared.

One second she was there. The next she wasn't.

Frost caught a glimpse of her throwing her arms up, but she was gone before he could reach out to grab her. She screamed.

Beside him, Denison also fell.

He didn't vanish as Lili had, but instead landed hard on his arse, and began scrabbling with his one hand, trying to find purchase.

Frost redirected his outstretched hand and clutched at Denison's shirt. He felt the man's weight shifting away, dragging him down. Only then did Frost see the fissure that jagged across the passage floor and ceiling: a deep crevice that went up several twists above them.

Denison felt impossibly heavy in his grasp, but he wasn't letting go. It was all Frost could do to brace himself and keep his own footing, as he attempted to haul the other man back from the brink.

Every muscle in his body burned.

His grip was slipping.

Gritting his teeth, Frost heaved again, and the stone beneath Denison crumbled away.

He dropped quickly into a prone position, spreading himself wide to lower his centre of gravity, and grabbed Dennison with a second hand, pulling him back.

Denison scooted away from the edge of the crevice, grunting and gasping as he moved. Frost realised why the other man felt so incredibly heavy: Denison had succeeded where he had failed, catching hold of Lili's arm as she had fallen.

Once both men were firmly on solid ground, Lili's rescue took only a few seconds. There were no congratulations or thanks. It was all they could do to lie flat, gasping until they'd caught their breath. Frost's heart was still pounding.

Lili took the light from Denison's hand, and began studying the rubble that lay strewn around them. "The stones..." she said, disbelieving. "They have been *cut*."

"Cut?" Denison asked.

"Look." She held up a square chunk of rock. "The break is not natural. See?"

"We're in a manmade cavern," Denison pointed out.

She shook her head, and then directed the light up, into the open space of the fissure that bisected the passage. "This is Roman brick, from the ruins of the old city of Verulamium. Such bricks were used in the construction of the original abbey. I think we're under the cathedral."

Frost peered up into the void. "Turn off the light," he urged.

She did, and after an initial moment of near-total darkness, Frost saw a faint glow no more than twenty metres above them. "She's right."

The sides of the fissure were nearly vertical, but the stone hadn't fractured cleanly. It was instead marred with jagged pockmarks and strange, bulbous protrusions; a near-perfect stepladder for their ascent out of the abyss. Frost edged around the end of the broken passage and started looking for a route. The crevice was about five metres across at the point where it fractured the tunnel, and a little wider overhead. But just a few metres to the left, it narrowed to the extent that Frost could brace his back against the wall on the far side, and make the climb as though walking up a chimney-stack.

It only took a few minutes.

Even before he reached the upper limit of the fissure, he saw that Lili was right.

After passing a chalky stratus, there was evidence of the old Norman era architecture, which had in turn employed building materials that dated back nearly two thousand years. Frost hauled himself above the level of the fissure and into a dimly lit room.

The crypt.

He saw immediately that the damage had torn open a fissure in the ceiling above—the floor of the church. He stood on a sarcophagus, assuming the dead man wouldn't mind, and boosted himself up. When the fissure had opened across the floor, it had damaged one of the ornate arches, creating a cascade of stone and masonry.

Frost took a moment to survey the enclosure, noting the tile floor and mostly unadorned white walls. A few steps away, on an elevated platform, he saw several rows of straight-backed wooden chairs were lined up with military precision, and beyond that, he saw an altar situated near the far wall, directly below an enormous, circular window. He could only see the decorative stained-glass panes because of the moon. It was an eerie effect.

Opposite the altar was an open area, and beyond that, more rows of chairs, along with racks containing prayer books and scripture. At the far end he could just make out a balcony that ran beneath five long, vertical windows. Each window was topped in an elaborate Gothic arch. Although the area was vast, with a high, vaulted ceiling, the seating area seemed quite small. They'd most likely broken through into one of the chapels, not the cathedral proper.

He cut short his recce to help Lili up into the chapel.

As he took her hand, a voice echoed in the spacious enclosure: "What are you doing in here?"

Frost whirled defensively, going for the Browning, but before he could draw the weapon, he saw the man behind the voice: a middle-aged man wearing khakis and a souvenir T-shirt. He was on the stairs that led from the far balcony, staring down the length of the room in horror at the damaged arch. *One of the cathedral caretakers*, Frost guessed, no doubt drawn by the sound of the collapse.

Frost eased his hand away from the pistol, and beckoned the man closer. "The floor gave way. My friends are down there."

The newcomer's brows creased in irritation, but he did not repeat his question as he hastened over to lend a hand. Frost finished hauling Lili up, and got his first good look at her since their flight from the gunmen had begun. She was almost unrecognizable beneath a coating of dust and sweat. She looked like a refugee from hell itself. He probably didn't look much better.

While Frost and the other man helped Denison up out of the fissure, Lili looked around, and immediately recognised where they were. "This is the north transept, the oldest part of the abbey to survive, built almost a thousand years ago." She turned to Denison as he crawled out of the barrow and sprawled out on the tiled floor. "The original Benedictine abbey must have been situated above the entrance to the burial site."

Their anonymous benefactor looked askance at her. "I see you're familiar with the history of the abbey church. Now, perhaps you can explain what you're doing here. And how this happened?" His gesture swept from the fallen arch to the crevice.

Frost would have been content to let Denison and Lili come up with a suitable lie, but before anyone could speak, a loud *bang* echoed through the hall, and a moment later, two men rushed out of the shadows along the west side of the transepts.

Frost recognised one of them: he'd pounded him into the pavement outside the Royal Garden.

Both men ran with handguns out. The vaulted ceiling had amplified their single, wild shot, until it sounded like another grenade going off.

Trouble had once more found them.

"*Down!*" Frost yelled.

He drew the Browning even as he took his own advice, but the unnamed man, still struggling to understand the appearance of the three visitors and the inexplicable destruction of holy property, instinctively turned to meet the new arrivals. "What's the meaning of this?" he shouted, still not understanding. Frost reached out to pull the man to the ground, but in that instant, something warm and wet erupted from the man's torso. The thunder of gunfire filled the cathedral.

The man pitched backward, a volley of rounds sizzling through the air above Frost and the others, gouging enormous craters in the masonry walls.

Frost rolled away from the dead man, and returned fire from a prone position.

His heart slowed. He was deathly calm. There was no fear now. This was his world: a world he understood.

He triggered four rounds, and all of them found their target. The gunman he'd recognised jerked and twisted as Frost's shots stitched his groin and abdomen, making him dance as he died. The last bullet ripped through the man's neck, arterial blood fountaining from the wound.

Frost had already moved on.

He rolled again, seeking cover behind the rows of pews as bullets began hammering into the floor where he had been lying.

Frost high-crawled up the centre aisle, scrambling furiously on knees and elbows to remove himself from the remaining gunman's line of sight. He was trying to draw his attention away from Denison and Lili. Individual pews alongside him splintered as bullets struck the upright wooden backs, like tiny hammers. The air was suddenly alive with a swarm of flying splinters. The pews offered little real protection, and no real concealment; when he moved or turned his head, he had the impression of being able to see through them, to see his attacker's feet moving.

The man was turning away...

Going after the others....

"Bollocks," Frost grunted, and sprang to his feet. He fired two shots in the vicinity of where he guessed the man ought to be, but the shooter had anticipated the move. As Frost felt the Hi-power buck in his hands, he saw his opponent's muzzle flash. It was less than twenty metres away. It was harder to miss, even with the blood pumping and adrenalin driving the body. He twisted away, hurling himself into the pews—it was absolute agony as his side between hip and ribcage slammed down onto the hard edge of the pew backs. Even as he dove forward, he felt something bite into his upper left arm.

The flash of pain was quickly replaced by a cold numbness.

He'd taken a hit.

He didn't have time to think about it.

He fell hard, sprawling across the cold tiles, and was on the move immediately: crawling toward the south wall, despite the pain.

He crabbed forward, trying to catch a glimpse of the gunman through the maze of pew legs. Several of the benches had been knocked over, blocking his view; but just past one of these, he caught a flicker of movement.

Frost was a quick learner. Instead of popping up for a clear shot, he stayed prone, and aimed through the tangle of pew legs.

The gunman took another step, and Frost pulled the trigger.

There was an explosion of smoke and noise in the confined space, and Frost felt the sting of cordite in his eyes/ But through the ringing echoes of the Browning's report, he heard the gunman curse. Given the fact they were in a cathedral, Frost couldn't help but hope that the blasphemous string of cries brought on a divine smackdown. It didn't have to be showy: just a little help from on high.

Frost crabbed forward, keeping his head down, and in a few seconds, he reached the north aisle.

When he was clear of the pews, he placed his palms flat, and sprang up into a low crouch... or rather, that was his intent.

As he shifted his weight onto his arms, his left arm gave out, and he buckled and went down, face first into the floor.

Pain tore through his arm.

He couldn't surrender to it.

He rolled onto his good arm and levered himself up, and then duck-walked quickly down the aisle. As he moved, he realised that, while the curses and howls of pain from his foe had continued, there had been no further shots.

He edged around the last of the pews between them, and saw the gunman sitting on the floor near the centre aisle, back pressed up against the side of a pew. The man was clutching his knee, futilely trying to stem the flow of blood streaming through his fingers. When he saw Frost, he let go of the wound, releasing a pulse of blood, thick and sickly red-black. He reached out desperately for his pistol.

"Think of it as mercy," Frost said.

Two shots, one bullet in each of the man's shoulders.

The gunman rocked back with the impact, his arms useless.

His fingers dragged bloody streaks across the tiles and the discarded weapon. He couldn't grasp it, and even if, by some miracle, he could, there was no way he could pull the trigger. Frost scanned the immediate area looking for another threat, but found none. The area was secure. For now. Cautiously, he stood to full height, and advanced on the stricken gunman.

He was breathing rapidly through the pain of his wounds, and his eyes were filled with impotent rage as he watched Frost. Frost knelt in front of him.

"Fucker!" the gunman spat. The curse came with an aerosol spray of blood, and rivulets of red began leaking from the corners of the man's mouth.

Frost didn't see any injuries that could account for this. The idiot had probably bitten his tongue during the firefight.

The three wounds could well prove fatal without medical attention. It was supply and demand: while the heart kept pumping, the blood kept leaking out.

"Let me tell you a secret," Frost said, quite reasonably. "I couldn't care less whether you make it out of here. You tried to put me down. There's only one reason you're still breathing: I want to know who you're working for."

He placed the barrel of the Browning a few centimetres from the man's forehead.

The man's face twisted in a snarl.

His lips had already taken on a bluish tinge. His face grew paler with every passing second. He coughed. It became something else: a sound that might have been laughter. "You're a dead man walking, Ronan Frost. You're on the wrong side of this."

The words were no more than bravado.

"Who are you working for?" Frost repeated. "How did you find us?" His questions were met with the same death-rattle chuckle.

"Finish it. I'm not going to betray—" the coughing worsened.

Frost jammed the muzzle of the gun into one of the holes in the man's shoulder and yanked sideways, hard.

The man screamed.

Really screamed.

"So much for mercy. Now I have to hurt you."

"Kill me. You can't win. I'm not alone. Kill me and spend the rest of your life running. Do it. Kill me. You don't have the balls."

"You talk a lot, for a dead man," Frost said, and pistol-whipped the guy across the side of the face. He was unconscious before he hit the cathedral floor. Frost checked his pulse. Weak. But weak was better than non-existent.

You're on the wrong side of this.

An odd hiss crackled from under him. Frost patted the dead man down until he found the small hand-held radio clipped to his belt. "*Ghost one, report. The signal is stationary. Did you get them?*"

Understanding hit Frost like a slap.

He drew out his mobile phone, holding it like it was the enemy, and thumbed the button to turn it on. The signal status indicator in the corner of the display was unchanged—four bars, all full, but crossed with a diagonal slash.

They tracked my mobile.

But it was more than that.

He'd been cut off from Nonesuch.

The wrong side….

He became aware of Denison crouching down next to him, and Lili just a few steps away, her arms hugged tightly across her chest. "Give me your mobile phones," he barked.

Denison, eyes wide, handed his over without comment. Lili just shook her head. "I don't have one."

Frost laid Denison's phone on the floor next to his own, and used the butt of his pistol like a hammer to smash both devices until they were unrecognizable. Denison seemed to understand, and when Frost finished, he asked calmly: "Now what?"

Frost felt an unfamiliar anger seethe within him. He regarded his old friend. His old CO. He wanted the truth, and no one was telling it to him. "You tell me. Things are royally screwed here. No sword, people trying to kill us. I just shot two men, Tony, and I still have no idea *why*! I've been cut-off from my people. I'm out in the fucking cold, and we've got nothing to show for it but a mounting stack of bodies. So *you* tell me what we're supposed to do next."

"No!" Lili's utterance was both unexpected and unusually forceful. "Not nothing. The parchment I found... I know where the sword is."

"Oh, for fuck's sake—"

Denison cut Frost off. "Where?"

"The parchment was a letter from Octavian himself. That skeleton belonged to a centurion who had been ordered to take Labienus, along with an entire cohort, to Britain to recover the sword and bring it to Rome, where he would enshrine it in a temple. A temple that Julius Caesar had planned to build, and which Octavian, as Augustus Caesar, would eventually complete: the Temple of Mars Ultor." She was comfortable here, talking about this. It didn't involve guns or war crimes. It was familiar territory. Her expertise. "We assumed that the sword was still here, still buried with Nennius. We were wrong. Labienus found it, stole it from the tomb. The Britons killed the centurion, left his body there as a warning... but Labienus and the others escaped with their prize."

"What about all that business with the sword in the stone, and King Arthur?" Frost asked, trying to keep up.

"A false trail. As I said earlier, there may have been a sword in an anvil, which Vortigern claimed was the Crocea Mors. But the *real* sword was already long gone."

Denison repeated his question urgently. "Where?"

"Rome, of course. All roads lead to Rome."

Denison turned to Frost. "Ronan, you've done more for us than I could have hoped. I can't ask you to stick with us..." He let the implicit request hang in the air.

You're on the wrong side of this... He didn't even know what the sides were anymore, and yet, these killers had managed to use his mobile phone to track them to Saint Albans. His phone. That meant they knew *who* he was, knew *who* he worked for, which was something that even Denison didn't know.

The wrong side....

I've been sold out.

Some animal part of his brain railed against that notion. The old man wouldn't do that to him. But his rational mind couldn't see another alternative. Who else could have given him up? He gestured to the slumped form of the gunman. "He told me I was on the wrong side of this. Why did he say that, Tony? Make me understand. Otherwise I can't walk out of here with you."

"I've told you everything I know, Ronan."

"You haven't."

But there was no hint of duplicity in Denison's face.

Whether the whole business about the New World Order conspiracy was true or not, he clearly believed it was, and that was all that mattered.

"They're willing to kill us all to keep you from finding that sword," Frost pressed. "It's that important?"

Denison spread his hands. "I wouldn't have believed it either."

The wrong side....

What kind of crazy, fucked-up rabbit hole have I tumbled into?

"This isn't going to stop until we're dead."

"Or until we have that sword," Denison said.

Frost took a breath and let it out slowly. He felt a little light-headed, and realised that blood from the bullet wound in his arm had saturated his shirt sleeve beneath his jacket, and was now falling in fat drops on the tile. He turned to Lili. "You can find this Martian Temple?"

Lili nodded. "The Temple of Mars Ultor. I know where the ruins are. I *think* I know where the sword would have been kept."

Frost held her stare for a moment before looking to Denison. "Rome, then."

ELEVEN
ROADS THAT LEAD TO ROME

Then, Rome, Italy—44 BCE

Titus Labienus watched nervously as a phalanx of horses rode toward him.

In the light of the half moon, he could make out little more than their silhouettes, but there was no mistaking the orderliness of the formation or the military bearing of the riders—these were soldiers.

Not just any soldiers, but the elite Praetorian Guard, Octavian's personal protectors; fiercely loyal, recruited from the very best the legions had to offer. And they were coming for him.

Not for the first time, he wondered if he had made a grave mistake in contacting Octavian. The young heir apparent had approved the idea of sending a quest to Britain in order to recover Caesar's sword, and had even directed Labienus to travel with Marcus' cohort of legionaries, but he had not changed the terms of Labienus' imprisonment; the former tribune was still nominally under house arrest, still considered an enemy of Rome. The message was implicit: his status would not change unless the quest was successful.

Or until he was dead.

Labienus gripped the leather sheath in both hands. I've kept my part of the bargain. Will Octavian honour his?

Octavian knew that he had succeeded, knew what he carried, and yet he had not invited Labienus into the city for a formal reception. Instead, he had demanded this clandestine meeting.

He told himself that Octavian was merely being cautious, but part of him wondered if it would not have been wiser for him to cast his lot in with the senators—men who would have honoured his ill-advised decision to stand with Pompey against the self-styled dictator of Rome. Or, better: to simply take his prize and disappear, starting a new life somewhere far from Rome. Africa, perhaps.

Too late for that now.

The horsemen surrounded him and he felt a new flush of fear as the powerful animals closed in. He could feel their hot breath on his neck. They circled him. The riders gazed down from a position of overwhelming strength. Round and around. Dizzying. But made no move against him.

Then, one of them dismounted.

"Titus!"

He knew the voice, though it had been many years since they had travelled together, and the boy had grown into a man. Octavian.

Labienus stretched out his right hand, offering the customary gesture of friendship and peace. "My lord."

Octavian did not return the salute, but instead clasped a hand to Labienus' shoulder and guided him out of the circle of horsemen. "You have returned alone, Titus?"

"I have, lord. A great many things happened on the road."

Octavian stared at the sheathed blade that Labienus still clutched in his left hand, held protectively against his breast. "I would hear your tale."

Labienus nodded, and began speaking.

*

His memories of Britain were memories of war. Ten years earlier, he had ridden at the front of an army, spent his nights in a military encampment surrounded by a sea of hardened warriors. In that respect, Labienus' recollections of Britain were little different than any of the other battlefields on which he had fought.

Now, accompanied only by sixty legionaries instead of thousands, he felt as though he were seeing the place for the first time.

The journey across Gaul had been unremarkable. The news of Caesar's assassination had reached the far flung settlements, but the governors and garrison commanders were wisely biding their time, waiting to see who would emerge as Rome's next leader. No one wanted to tip their hand too soon. They told no one their true purpose, and when asked, Marcus had indicated only that their mission to Britain was diplomatic in nature, which was understood to mean that they were being sent to spy on the Britons, hence the small numbers.

They crossed the channel on a trade vessel, and were met by an envoy from Mandubracias. News of their mission had preceded them. Mandubracias had not forgotten the role of the Roman legions in making him king of Trinovantes, and affirmed his friendship with Rome and Julius Caesar's heir, but remained wary. An uneasy peace existed between the Trinovantes and the Catuvellauni, but if Cassivelaunus believed that the Romans were negotiating with his former enemy, it might mean renewed hostilities between the island's two dominant tribes.

Under the pretext of reassuring the Catuvellauni leader that Rome had no interest in upsetting the balance of power on the island, they would be able to journey unmolested to Cassivelaunus' stronghold, which as luck would have it, lay only a short distance from the crypt of Prince Nennius and the sword of Julius Caesar.

Cassivelaunus had not forgotten Rome either, and while he recounted his memories of the battles with Caesar in warmly nostalgic terms, even expressing sorrow at the news of the assassination, there was no mistaking the undercurrent of enmity in the hospitality of his hall. The message was clear: *Be on your way, and do not return.*

On the eve of their departure, Marcus and Labienus stole from the fortress under cover of darkness and made their way on foot to the sacred hill where the Catuvellauni buried their dead.

Once away from the settlement, they did not have to worry about attracting notice; the superstitious Britons may have insisted on preserving the bodies of their dead, but they kept them at a healthy distance. The two men made their way up the rutted wagon trail to the top of the hill, where they found the entrance to the Hall of the Dead.

Hidden from the view of the distant fortress, they risked lighting a small lamp before venturing inside.

Labienus wasn't a superstitious man, and he'd seen more than his share of corpses, but those were always the freshly dead—men cut down in battle, victims of disease or accidents.

This was different.

The claustrophobic tunnels of the crypt and the oppressive stench of decay were an assault on his senses. His anxiety quickened as he ventured deeper. He began to see figures moving in the shadows cast by the flickering lamplight.

The dead were restless.

Of course they are, Labienus thought. They were left to rot, when they should have been cremated so their souls could journey to Elysium. Pity them. Do not fear them. Pity them.

But that was easier thought than put into practice. He hurried, searching the burial niches one after the other until at last, he found the one corpse that had not been interred with a crude sword of iron.

He looked at the dead man, remembering him in all of his glory on the battlefield.

It was always so hard to reconcile the bones of a man with the man himself.

Now he was reduced. Brought to nothing. His flesh had rotted through and fed the maggots and worms until nothing more than bones remained.

Labienus bowed his head in respect, and whispered, "Well met old enemy. Sleep on."

He hastily pried the *gladius* from Nennius' bony grasp, and without another word, he crept back up the tunnels into the air, then down the hill again, the moon on their heels.

In the morning, they departed as planned, confident that their intrusion would go unnoticed, probably forever, and rode south, following the river. It was a two-day ride at a leisurely pace, but with their prize in hand, they rode hard, pushing the horses to exhaustion, stopping only when the darkness made safe travel impossible.

As the legionaries tended to the horses and established a night watch, Labienus stretched out on the ground, and with the sword clutched protectively in his arms, fell into a troubled slumber.

*

He awakened with a start.

The camp was bathed in the light of a nearly-full moon.

One of the soldiers guarding the perimeter looked his way. They exchanged a nod, and then the man resumed his vigil as if nothing were wrong.

Doesn't he know what's about to happen? Labienus thought, frantically.

But the legionary hadn't shared his premonition of danger.

Labienus pushed himself to his feet, and went in urgent search through the sleeping men for Marcus.

A chilling war cry broke the silence.

A storm of death was unleashed on the camp.

Sling stones and spears whistled out of the surrounding woods, ringing against armour and shield, crunching into bone and flesh.

The legionaries rallied, forming a shield barrier, but a dozen of their number were already down.

Labienus wore no armour, but he was not unarmed.

He hefted Caesar's sword, and stood his ground, waiting for the attackers to rush out of the darkness.

"Titus," Marcus urged. "We cannot fail. You must take the sword. Go. Get it to Rome."

"Flee?" Labienus understood the other man's reasoning, but attempting to retreat through the dark, unfamiliar terrain was every bit as dangerous as staying to fight.

"Take ten men," Marcus ordered. "I will hold them here, and if I am able, join you again on the road. And if not, I will see you in Elysium. Now, go."

Labienus gripped the hilt of the sword. Was this why the gods had roused him? Not to fight, but so that he could escape with the sword?

Who could ever truly know the will of the gods?

He didn't argue with the warrior. The unseen attackers had them surrounded, but Labienus' protectors mounted and broke through—at a cost of two more dead—and attempted to gallop south following the river. The treacherous darkness made it impossible. One horse went down, stumbling on a tree root, and crushed its rider in the fall. They left the injured man there and kept going. He would die on the roadside, alone. The man didn't beg for mercy. He promised to delay the enemy if he could.

The sound of the nearby battle ceased.

In the ensuing silence, Labienus experienced another premonition of danger. He looked at his remaining seven men. "They will come for us."

The legionary leading the group stared back at him, the moonlight giving his face the pallor of a corpse. "We will not escape," he said, his voice cold and emotionless. Then he gripped Labienus' shoulder earnestly. "But you might. Let us stand here and buy you time with our lives."

*

"You, alone, survived?" Octavian asked. It sounded like an accusation of cowardice.

Labienus nodded, his face burning. "The only way to honour their sacrifice was to fulfil our mission. I hid in the woods until the battle was done. I stayed there for two full days, not daring to move, living on dirt and grubs, as the Britons plundered and desecrated the dead. Thereafter, I travelled only at night and made my way to shore where I found passage to Gaul."

Octavian shook his head as if Labienus had missed the point. "But there are none alive, save yourself, who know the truth of what you were doing? No one else knows about the sword?"

"None, Lord." Labienus did not have to consider this for even a moment. Secrecy had been paramount, and not just because of the fear that enemies might try to take the sword from them. Labienus still recalled why Julius Caesar had denied him permission to retrieve the sword after losing it to Nennius ten years earlier. *They will believe it is the sword that has conquered them, not the man who wields it.*

That dictum held true for Octavian as well, perhaps more so, for unlike his predecessor, he had not yet proven himself as a leader of men.

Caesar had also said something else. *It's only a sword.*

That, Labienus knew, had been a lie.

But it didn't matter.

He had accomplished the mission and he wanted nothing more than to return home. Perhaps Octavian would reward him—at the very least, he hoped his banishment would be at an end—but right now, all that mattered was being rid of the infernal burden.

He held the sword out, presenting it to Octavian.

And that was when he experienced the premonition again.

Octavian noticed it as well. "You've seen this moment before?"

Labienus nodded. "Just before we were attacked." He had not described the premonition in detail, fearing that Octavian would think him mad, but now the omission was irrelevant.

Octavian closed his hand around the hilt and slowly drew the sword from its sheath. Even in the darkness, it was a glorious thing. Truly, a thing of beauty. It felt like an extension of his arm, his spirit coursing out through his hand into the metal, joining them.

"Caesar spoke often of this," Octavian said, gazing upon the naked blade. "The Sword of Mars. The man who wields it cannot be defeated in battle. It warns when danger or treachery is at hand."

Labienus gaze darted past Octavian, into the darkness where the Praetorian Guard waited. "Is there danger here, lord?"

"Of a sort. The danger that comes when one's weaknesses are exposed. The gods will guide me to victory; I will become *imperator*. Then, I will build a temple in their honour to guard gifts such as this. But no one can know that I owe my victories to it."

"No one will ever learn of it from me," Labienus assured him.

"I know." Octavian smiled, and then thrust the sword through Labienus' heart.

PART TWO
THE SWORD OF MARS

TWELVE
DAUGHTER

Now, Saint Albans—2216 UTC

They slipped away from the cathedral just as the local police began arriving on the scene. They made their way into town on foot, moving quickly. They didn't talk. The hired VW was abandoned. They didn't steal a car; doing so would only tip their hand when it was found. They didn't want anyone knowing where they'd gone. So for the second time that night, the anonymity of public transport would help them make their escape.

They had emerged from the cathedral filthy, bedraggled, and in Frost's case, bleeding from the wound to his left bicep. The first order of business was cleaning up. Frost's injury wasn't bad, at least in his own estimation—he'd certainly suffered worse—but a trail of blood would attract attention. After meandering through residential neighbourhoods, putting nearly three kilometres between themselves and the cathedral, they found an all-night chemist. Denison went in alone to buy some clothes and first aid supplies, while Lili and Frost stayed outside, concealed by the shadows.

Frost struggled out of his jacket and began gingerly peeling his shirt, sticky with drying blood, away from the wound. Seeing his difficulty, Lili took over. She had a delicate touch, but did not seem too squeamish, even when the wound reopened.

"Sorry," she murmured.

"No worries." The pain was nowhere near intolerable. One didn't come up through the Paras and the SAS without learning how to deal with a few cuts and bruises. It was a through-and-through. It had barely clipped the meat. It'd need stitching, but that could wait.

On the wrong side...Frost believed that Denison was being honest, but he couldn't shake the nagging feeling he wasn't saying everything.

As he watched Lili carry his ruined shirt over to a street corner rubbish bin, it occurred to him that he hadn't really had a chance to talk to her at all. They'd been running pretty much from the moment they'd met, and on any subject unrelated to ancient history, she seemed about as talkative as a lamppost.

"Some night," he said. As icebreakers went it wasn't particularly sophisticated, but it beat spelling it out gunshot by gunshot. "You holding up?"

She shrugged. "This is not the first time someone has tried to kill me."

"I imagine your father made some enemies when he decided to support the NATO intervention."

Her eyes narrowed and she looked away. "My father's actions during the war were... shameful."

Touched a nerve.

Frost recalled that Kristijan Pavic's trial in the World Court was nearly finished. Closing arguments had already been made, and the verdict was expected within the week. *Odd that she's with Tony, looking for some rusty old relic, and not at her father's side,* he realised.

"I've followed his trial. For what it's worth, I believe he'll be found not guilty."

"Not guilty?" She made no effort to hide her contempt. "He is *absolutely* guilty. Guilty of betraying his people; choosing to protect our enemies and work with—" Her nose wrinkled in disgust as she nodded at Frost— "foreigners interfering where they had no business."

Frost said nothing.

Lili was angry with her father for *not* doing the things of which he'd been accused.

She was angry that he'd worked with NATO to stop the bloodshed.

The implications of that appalled him.

Hadn't she seen the mass graves where thousands of ethnic Albanians had been massacred and covered over by bulldozers?

Didn't she feel anything for the women and girls who had been raped and brutalised as part of a deliberate campaign of ethnic cleansing?

But part of him understood.

He had grown up surrounded by people whose convictions left them with a completely altered sense of reality. It wasn't hatred. It was deeper, darker, than that.

"If you feel that way, why are you working with Tony?"

"Don't mistake me: I have no anger toward him, or you for that matter. You were soldiers following orders." Despite the evident passion she felt for the subject, Lili's tone had lost some of its fire. She managed to regain some of her composure, and was quickly her prickly self again. When she continued, she sounded less like a true believer and more like a history professor giving a lecture. "Did your superiors tell you who you were *protecting*? The Kosovo Liberation Army were terrorists. Your government accused the Serbs of ethnic cleansing; do you know what the KLA was trying to accomplish? An ethnically pure Albanian Kosovo. They attacked, raped and massacred Serbs, Romanies... anyone who was not Albanian. They used children as soldiers. They trafficked in narcotics, even sold the organs of their prisoners to raise money for their war. But *who* did your government choose to support? The KLA. Because of politics. Because it was convenient. And that is why I am working with Tony. It is convenient."

That stopped Frost. "Convenient? I know what Tony is after—or what he says he's after; so what's your angle?"

She raised an eyebrow. "I am a historian. Classical Rome is my area of expertise. Isn't that enough?"

Frost shrugged. "Hardly. Not in my world. It might explain your interest, but not why you were so eager to play Lara Croft tonight."

Her lip curled in something that might have been a smile, in another life. "When that man attacked us in the parking garage, I realised the urgency of the situation."

Frost wasn't convinced.

He shook his head.

He recalled how, following their rendezvous at Heathrow, she—not Denison—had insisted that they proceed immediately to Saint Albans.

But before he could call bullshit on her, Denison returned, bearing his purchases: souvenir T-shirts to at least partially camouflage their soiled and battered condition; antiseptic and bandages for Frost's arm; and a disposable pre-paid burner phone. Frost would need the latter to arrange for one of his contacts to supply them with forged travelling papers.

"It is ironic, really," Lili continued as she tended to Frost's wound. "The sword being in Rome. I was so very close to it, and didn't even know it."

Denison raised an eyebrow, but said nothing.

"What makes you so sure it's there? I can accept that they came back and stole it from that tomb, but getting it out of the country couldn't have been easy. And you said yourself that, until you found that first letter, there was no evidence the sword even *existed*. Maybe it's just gone? Lost on the way back to Rome. Even if they got it off the mainland, their ship could have sunk...the sword could be lying on the bottom of the Channel, for all we know."

She shook her head. "You don't understand the politics of the time. The proof is in Octavian's success. Here was a man thought by his peers to be pliable... even weak. And yet, through a combination of military and political cunning, he succeeded in becoming Rome's first and, I would say, greatest emperor."

"He was Caesar's son; maybe it was in his blood."

Lili shook her head. "No. Octavian wasn't related to Julius Caesar by blood. He was formally adopted after Caesar's assassination in order to legally establish his position as Caesar's heir. It is true that Caesar may have seen something in the boy, and he certainly would have cultivated the qualities necessary to someday rule an empire, but I think Octavian had something else."

"A magic sword that established his divine right to rule?" Frost glanced over at Denison as he said it, and saw his old friend nodding thoughtfully.

"In this case, it's the truth. The Crocea Mors was said to be the sword of the god Mars. With that sword in his possession, and a promise to place it in a magnificent temple dedicated to Mars, Octavian would have gained the support of the priests of the war god, which in turn would have given him considerable influence with the legions. This may even explain why Marc Antony was willing to set aside his own ambitions in order to share power with Octavian."

"Lili," Denison interjected. "You said that you were very close to the sword without realising it; what did you mean by that?"

"I wrote my doctoral dissertation on Augustus. I spent a great deal of time at historical sites related to Rome's first emperor. The Musei Capitolini—the Capitoline Museum—has an extensive collection of artefacts from the Augustine Forum where the Temple of Mars Ultor was located."

"And the sword is there? In a *museum*?" Frost felt his ire rising. After everything they had gone through, the possibility that the object of their search might actually be in a climate-controlled display case, in a well-lit conservatory, in a modern city, made him feel used.

Then Lili took a deep breath, like a doctor about to give an ailing patient a terminal diagnosis. "It's not that simple. I'll explain everything when we get there. I promise."

THIRTEEN
THE IMPOSSIBLE

Nonesuch Manor—2249 UTC

Sir Charles jabbed a finger down on the speaker button as soon as the caller ID came up on the display. When he spoke, it was with an air of practiced calm that was decidedly at odds with his present mood. "Konstantin, my boy. So good of you to finally check in. Would you care to debrief us?"

The question was almost sincere. Sir Charles knew exactly where Khavin was; Lethe had tracked the Russian's mobile south through London, where it had disappeared for more than half an hour, only to reappear in Calais. More to the point, he knew what the big Russian had been doing, too, but he wanted to give him the chance to explain his actions.

"I was looking into something," Konstantin answered.

"Ah. And were you successful in your endeavours?"

"I believe so. I am following up on it now," Konstantin said, steering carefully away from the subject. "Is there any word from Frost?"

Sir Charles grimaced, glad it wasn't a video phone, and kept his tone neutral. "He is also 'looking into something.'"

"I see."

There was a maddening pause, and Sir Charles finally cracked: "Damn it, Konstantin, you're the one who called me. I can't help you if you don't tell me what you need." When Khavin did not immediately relent, Sir Charles took a different tack. "There was a disturbance at Clarendon House tonight."

"Yes?"

"Some chap claiming to be a police inspector assaulted one of the members of the protection retinue assigned to a certain royal highness."

"That takes some audacity."

"Indeed it does. The police circulated a photograph of the assailant, captured from CCTV inside Clarendon, but as of now, no one is quite sure who he is."

Konstantin waited for more. When it didn't come, he asked: "Do you want me to look into it?"

"No need. Shortly after the word went out, Clarendon House advised the police that it was a false alarm. It's as if the incident never happened."

"Convenient." Khavin let out a sigh.

"Indeed. So why *have* you called?"

"I need information on David Habersham."

Sir Charles nodded across the room to Lethe, who was already running a search. A list of hits flashed on the plasma screen monitor mounted on the wall. "Too wide a search," Sir Charles muttered.

"Limit it to British subjects. Possible nationalist connections. Last known location, most likely the Netherlands."

Sir Charles nodded absently at the last comment. Now he understood why Khavin was in France. He'd taken the train under the channel, and was probably even now waiting for a connection to take him up to the Netherlands. The Russian didn't fly if he could help it. And border control in Europe was so lax with the Schengen agreement in place now. You could ride from the boot of Italy into the Arctic Circle and down through the Low Countries into England without showing any ID until you hit mainland Britain.

The screen refreshed, and instead of countless results returning leads in different directions, Sir Charles saw that all of the hits referred to a single man: David Ambrose Habersham. Born in Cardiff. Dividing his time between a modern London condominium on the Isle of Dogs, and a country villa near The Hague in the Netherlands. Habersham was the president of GreenWave Enterprises, a leading researcher into alternative energy production, and in that capacity, had become both an advisor and a close personal friend of a certain member of the royal family. The two men had been photographed together on numerous occasions, leaving little question in Sir Charles' mind that this was the man Khavin was looking for.

"Send it to him," Sir Charles said, with a nod to Lethe. Then he continued in a louder voice. "Can I take it that you have found a connection between Mr Habersham and the Four Evangelists?"

"It's only hearsay at this point. Certainly not enough to exonerate Denison, or clear Frost."

Sir Charles hid his disappointment, if only from Lethe. "Keep at it. And Koni...while I do thank you for trying to insulate me from your, ah, endeavours tonight, please don't do anything like that *ever again*. It's going to take Mr Lethe a month of Sundays to get your likeness out of the Secret Service database now."

"I have no idea what you are talking about, Sir," Khavin replied and killed the connection.

The old man continued to stare at the monitor, wondering if this new discovery would be the thread to lead them out of the labyrinth, or another maddening false trail.

"Habersham is on Six's watch list," Lethe said.

The old man would trust Khavin's instincts on this, although that didn't make him feel any less helpless. And he hated feeling helpless more than anything. It was a consequence of the fact he was bound to the wheelchair now. In his mind, he could still walk like a giant. He was still waiting for the fallout from the Russian's brazen intrusion at Clarendon House. They'd obviously identified him as the intruder; that Carruthers hadn't already set the phone lines on fire was ominous, to say the least.

At least the GPS signal from Frost's mobile had gone dark—his last known location, Saint Albans. There were conflicting reports of a bomb blast and a shooting, and at least three dead, though none of the victims matched the descriptions for Frost or Denison. So Frost knew he'd been cut loose. The old man hoped to Christ it was enough of a head start to keep him alive.

And Nonesuch was clean.

He had followed Carruthers' orders explicitly, cutting Frost off from all communication. With Frost gone dark, it was inevitable that the man from Vauxhall Cross would come around again, this time demanding that they set the dogs on one of their own.

He wasn't looking forward to the confrontation. He would refuse, of course.

Frost was better than good. Finding him, even if he were inclined to do so, would be as good as impossible.

And yet...Despite what Control had said, Frost was in the best position to investigate Denison, and if necessary, take appropriate action. Sir Charles did not doubt the Irishman's ability to put duty ahead of friendship. Not for a second.

But that was secondary: Frost needed to know that he wasn't on his own.

Not now, not ever.

"Enough," the old man rumbled. "Mr Lethe, I have a new task for you."

"Lay it on me."

"Ronan needs to know what we have learned. You *must* find a way to make contact, and I don't care how you do it, short of starting a war; and even then, I might not complain too loudly if it gets the job done." Carruthers' threat echoed in his mind. *If you interfere, you're finished. Ogmios is finished.* "But it would be good if you could do so in a manner that cannot be traced back to us."

"His mobile's off. He's knows they were using it to track him. He won't turn it on again. And he won't check in, because he knows we must have turned him over to Six."

"Like I said, I don't care how you do it. Be creative," he gave the young man a reassuring nod. "That's why I hired you, Jude. To do the impossible."

FOURTEEN
THE PATH OF MARS

Rome—0235 Local (0135 UTC)

It took just an hour and forty minutes for them to travel from London to Rome: four hours after emerging from the ancient burial warren underneath Holywell Hill.

It took longer for Frost's man to deliver quality documentation than it did to fly. The forgeries were good. They had the bio-imprint stuff. All they needed was a photo for the facial recognition scanners, and even that didn't take more than a couple of hours to pull together.

As the plane touched down at Leonardo da Vinci International Airport, Frost found himself wondering how long it had taken Labienus to make the same journey. A damn sight longer was the only answer he could come up with.

Lili would probably know, but Frost didn't feel like asking her.

He was tired beyond belief, and under a layer of gauze bandages, his arm was throbbing in time with his heartbeat. The physical stress was nothing compared with the looming uncertainty about what was really going on, and just what the hell he was getting himself into. He'd been compromised—cut loose from Nonesuch. He couldn't believe they'd abandon him. But he could well believe they'd have to protect themselves—and probably him in the process, by letting him run. That was the only thing that made sense. This didn't change anything. He was on his own. The only people he trusted were back in London. If he survived the night, and somehow succeeded in finding the Crocea Mors, then what?

Frost couldn't think about that right now.

One of the core tenets of his SAS training was focus on the immediate goals. Anything else ran the risk of letting the enormity of the big picture overwhelm and paralyze. So right now, his world was reduced to the sword.

A Fiat 500 waited for them in the rental car pick-up area.

Lili, citing her experience as a one-time resident of the mad Italian metropolis—and more than passingly familiar with the crazy one-way system, the narrow cuts between buildings too tight to be called roads, the endless darting and weaving kids on their Piagios—suggested that she be allowed to drive. Frost was in no mood to argue the point, and didn't care about calling shotgun, so he took the rear seat, where he could stretch his legs out and, with any luck, catch a few more minutes of downtime before the next phase of Denison's crazy treasure hunt got underway.

The ride from the airport, which was situated on the Mediterranean coast, into the city proper took closer to an hour than the promised half an hour: time which, for Frost at least, passed in the blink of an eye.

"*Mausoleo di Augusto,*" Lili announced, startling Frost out of his shallow sleep. "The Mausoleum of Augustus."

He lifted his head and peered out the window, but there was little to see.

Like any city, Rome never went completely dark or quiet, but at three in the morning, it was about as restful as it ever got. Although the area behind them was ablaze with artificial light, the foreground, illuminated by the Fiat's headlights, showed only stacked bricks and a scattering of trees.

"Augustus' tomb?" Denison asked. "You think the sword might be buried with him?"

She shook her head. "The mausoleum was a monument commissioned by Augustus himself, and was meant to hold not only his remains, but those of the imperial family and other nobles. It was a common practice for kings to build their own tombs while they were still alive. But unlike many other cultures of the day, the Romans practiced cremation and did not bury their dead with grave goods. The mausoleum was intended to be only a repository for the ashes of Augustus and his family, and of course, a monument to his greatness.

"However, in the year 410, armies under Alaric the Visigoth sacked Rome and stole the golden urn containing Augustus' ashes, so it is no longer the last resting place of Rome's first emperor. If the Crocea Mors had been there with Augustus, it would have been pillaged as well."

"Great. So we've just flown a thousand miles in the middle of the night to a pillaged tomb? Explain it to me. Please. Because I'm bloody tired." Frost rubbed his face. He wasn't lying. He was bone tired.

"The mausoleum has other secrets." She opened the door. "Come. I will show you."

Lili led them past a row of trees and up a shadow-shrouded gravel path that ran alongside the remains of a crumbling masonry wall. They finally arrived at a wrought-iron gate that blocked entry to the other side of the wall. Lili switched on her Mini-MagLite LED torch. They had each purchased one at the airport gift shop, expecting to do most of their hunting in the dark. They were better prepared than they had been at Saint Albans.

Frost would have preferred something with a little more offensive capability; he'd been forced to leave his Browning behind. There was no way he could have got it through customs, and he didn't have a carry permit or any sort of permission under his false ID. He didn't like the fact that the killers would be able to pick up their trail again and he would be as good as naked in front of them. But he didn't have a choice.

"We will need to climb over the gate," Lili said, gesturing with her torch. The light darted up the wrought iron and back down again.

"Maybe we should try this in the morning," Denison offered.

She shook her head. "The site was closed to the public years ago. We'll only attract more attention if we do this in the daytime." Without further explanation, she worked her foot into the space between the bars of the gate and pulled herself up and over the top in one, smooth movement. Frost was impressed, but didn't say anything.

With a shrug directed at Frost, Denison followed her lead, but needed Frost to cup his hands and boost him up over the top. As soon as he was over, Frost himself clambered onto the gate. His ascent took longer than the others because of his arm, but even so, the gate posed no great hardship. In a few seconds, he was following Lili and Denison up the stone steps leading into the mausoleum.

The stairs fed into an impossibly tight corridor that, after Frost turned slightly sideways to squeeze through, led through an enclosed building—the mausoleum itself—within an open, circular courtyard. Frost could see scattered stones in the glow of Lili's light, but little else. She moved unhesitatingly into the centre of the courtyard, where another circular structure stood. She slipped into another narrow passageway, which forced Frost to remember that two thousand years ago, Romans were not exactly giants. The passage was framed by an arched opening. She shone her light on an enormous decorative column in the centre of the room, revealing a small enclosure in the very heart of it.

"Augustus' urn was kept there," she explained. "After the Visigoths raided the monument, it was, for a time, converted into a castle. But like so much else during the Middle Ages, it fell into ruin. In the 1930s, Mussolini, believing himself to be Augustus reborn, began restoring the site. That is when this was discovered."

She circled around the column reaching a point that was almost directly opposite the funerary room. With her torch tucked under one arm, she pressed her palms flat against the stone surface. There was a gentle scraping noise, and then a section of the column began to move, sliding inward, exposing an opening about a metre in diameter and half as deep.

"Now, I wasn't expecting that," Frost said.

Lili ignored him and squeezed through the narrow opening. Denison produced his own MagLite and followed her inside, leaving Frost to bring up the rear.

"Did I mention that I really don't like confined spaces?"

No one answered him.

Just beyond the concealed door, a set of steps had been cut into the volcanic rock that formed the foundation of the mausoleum.

The descending passage was cramped. Again, Frost was forced to turn sideways, but this time he had to duck as well, to avoid cracking his skull off the ceiling. Romans were also short, he realised. The scene felt like a replay of the misadventure under Holywell Hill, but unlike that ancient barrow, this place had not simply been sealed up and forgotten. Lili certainly seemed to know her way around, and the realisation made him uneasy. But then, he was by nature a suspicious soul.

He followed their lights down.

And down.

After about a hundred steps, the passage flattened out and continued in a straight line, leading, Frost thought, to the southwest. The walls were damp to the touch, and the air was musty. It had that old smell of air that wasn't breathed very often. Frost recalled that they had crossed the Tiber River shortly before reaching the mausoleum. The chamber was almost certainly below the water table. During heavy rains, the passage was probably flooded. *So where did the water drain to?* He could make out the curve of the arched ceiling overhead in the glow of the handheld lights, but little else.

Then to his surprise, they reached an intersecting passage.

Lili kept going straight.

Another fifty metres further on, she turned left at a second intersection.

Frost kept the twists and turns in his mind.

He wanted his exit strategy in place.

The narrow tunnel forced them to move single file and made conversation impossible—not that anyone was talking. Frost had only the glow of his companions' torches, what little of it wasn't blocked by their silhouettes, to guide him. Step by step further into the dank tunnel his sense of unease increased.

In Saint Albans, they'd had Denison's geophys map, incomplete as it was, to show the way. Here they had nothing. Lili had told them a story and led them into the dark. She knew her way around this subterranean labyrinth with a level of familiarity that could only come with a lot of time spent down here, but that didn't make him feel any better about following her. If the Crocea Mors was here, in a place that Lili obviously knew, why hadn't she recognised it from the start? These questions echoed through Frost's mind as he trudged on in solitary silence, wishing he still had the Browning.

Lili navigated through several more turns, which grew progressively tighter until they were moving in near-absolute darkness, following their way with their hands, until with unexpected abruptness, they emerged into a large circular chamber which likewise had been cut from the volcanic rock that formed Rome's foundation.

Stairs had been carved into the wall, spiralling around the chamber and ascending into the gloom overhead, but Lili's objective was in the centre of the room: a series of round platforms, each more than a metre high, rose in tiers, culminating in a dais that towered more than twenty metres above their heads.

"We now are beneath the ruins of the Temple of Mars Ultor," she said, reverently. This, finally, was a holy place she had respect for, he realised. She climbed up to the dais. "Mars the Avenger. The temple was built to commemorate Augustus' victory over the assassins of Julius Caesar, as well as his recovery of battle standards lost in the war with the Parthians.

"This room is the *sacellum* where those standards and the other sacred relics of Mars were kept when not on display. Augustus' mausoleum lies on the northern edge of the Campus Martius—the Field of Mars—where in the days of the Republic, the legions would assemble. When he commissioned the mausoleum, Augustus also ordered the creation of an underground passage that would connect the temple to the Field of Mars."

Denison gazed up at Lili in open admiration, but Frost's instincts wouldn't shut up. Something was off about the whole thing. It was a charade. He drew close to his old friend. "Something's wrong here."

Denison looked back blankly.

"This isn't like the tombs at Saint Albans," Frost whispered. "This place has been used...*recently.*"

Lili must have overheard his whisper. "The Path of Mars and this treasure vault are not well known, but neither are they a guarded secret."

"If it's so well known, then how can anything of value be left unfound? I'm not buying it."

She shrugged. "Come up and have a look for yourself."

Denison immediately clambered onto the high platform. Frost watched him go. There was nothing he could do to protect the man from twenty metres below him. With a sigh of resignation, he followed.

A large round structure, like a table or altar, occupied the centre of the dais. The top surface was flat, but a pattern of lines, like spokes of a wheel—twelve in all—radiated from a circle cut into the stone.

Lili shone her light onto the circle.

"A bronze statue of Mars the Avenger once stood here, standing guard over the sacred relics."

"And the Crocea Mors was one of those relics?" Denison supposed.

"In the myths of Rome, Mars wielded a spear. You are familiar with his ancient symbol? A circle with an upraised spear point—it is also a universal symbol for the male gender."

"I thought that was supposed to be a penis," Frost muttered.

Lili ignored him. "In the time of Augustus, a spear said to be the Spear of Mars was kept in a shrine in the Regia, where the ancient kings of Rome lived. It was believed that, when the Republic faced great crisis, the spear would vibrate. It reportedly did so when Julius Caesar was assassinated. Following the victory of Augustus, the spear was moved to the new temple in the Forum, and safeguarded here. But there were other spears, too. The *Flamen Martialis*—the high priest of Mars—was attended to by the *Salii*: twelve young priests from patrician families. They would dress as warriors to perform the rituals of worship during the festival month of March—named for the war god—and when the legions embarked on a campaign or returned victorious. As part of their ritual attire, they each carried a replica of that spear."

Lili bent over the altar and gripped one of the wedged-shaped sections. With surprising ease, it slid back to reveal a void underneath. When she shone her light inside, it was reflected back in a glint of metal.

Denison, his eyes dancing in anticipation, took a step closer and with almost reverent deliberation, reached inside. When he withdrew his hand, his fingers were curled around a broad bladed spearhead, and his eager expression gave way to disappointment.

Lili leaned over the altar and began moving another of the wedge segments.

The opening was now large enough for Frost to see that the interior of the altar contained several of the Roman-style spears, their steel edges dulled by time. Most of them were immaculately restored.

"These don't look like ancient weapons."

"They were restored by a secret commission of historians and art experts in the 1930s," Lili insisted, pushing back yet another section to reveal even more blades. "On the orders of Mussolini himself, and cared for ever since by like-minded individuals dedicated to preserving the ways of the old gods. These are the ancient relics of Mars, used by the *Salii* in ancient Rome, and by their modern counterpart even to this day."

"Some kind of Mars cult?" Frost made no effort to hide his sarcasm.

"In a word, yes."

"And they just leave all this stuff here, where anyone can just wander in?"

"No one just wanders onto the Path of Mars," Lili spoke with an unusual degree of confidence. "It isn't exactly Via Cavour."

"I don't understand," Denison said. "What does any of this have to do with the Crocea Mors?"

She looked at him like he was a child. "The worship of Mars reached its zenith under Augustus. Within a hundred years of his death, Venus had become the favoured deity. This may be attributable to the changing demographics of both the city population and of the army. You see, in addition to being the god of war, Mars was also an agricultural deity. In the early Republic, the army was made up of citizens; they would plant their crops in the springtime, and then assemble on the Campus Martius to fight for the glory of Rome. They would pray to Mars both for success in battle and for a bountiful harvest to be waiting for them at home. But as the empire grew, the old ways changed. The worship of Mars made little sense to most Romans, who were neither farmers nor legionaries. By the second century, both the worship of Mars and the use of the Augustine Forum went into decline."

Lili paused, allowing the significance of what she'd just said sink in.

Frost wasn't sure he understood.

"There is nothing in the historical record regarding the disposition of the relics from the Temple of Mars Ultor. Everything kept here—the battle standards, the Spear of Mars, and yes, perhaps even the Crocea Mors—simply vanished from history."

Frost said nothing.

"You asked how I knew of this place; I'll tell you. My thesis advisor brought me here to witness the rites of the *Salii*. I knew nothing of the sword's origin then, the notion of it being Caesar's blade... And then we discovered the reference to it in the palimpsest. I was sure the sword was in England; it made sense, because it was where Caesar lost it. But *if* the sword was brought here, *if* it was kept with the other relics... then what happened to it?"

"Stolen," Frost answered. "Surely? You mentioned some invasion? Maybe they found this place, too? Possible?"

She shook her head. "No. If they had, history would have remembered it. You sack your enemy and rob their most sacred treasures, you ram it home, and you glory in it. You let the world know. So no, if those relics came back here, then I think those relics are still here. There must be secrets here that haven't been uncovered. There *must* be."

It sounded like she was clutching at straws, but Denison's eyes lit up as he finally understood what she was driving at. "A secret room."

"It is the only explanation. Someplace that neither Mussolini's experts, nor the modern keepers of the old ways, even thought to look for."

"Okay, so if we believe this: where do we look?"

Lili made a sweeping gesture, as though to say *everywhere*, then turned her attention back to the circular receptacle containing the spears.

Frost turned on his own light and began scrutinizing the dais, not sure exactly what he was looking for. The outer ring had been decorated with carvings, each corresponding to one of the wedge-shaped sections. "You said there were twelve of these priests—"

"The *Salii*."

"Is that important? The number twelve?"

"Twelve has always been an important number," Denison offered. "Especially in religion. There were twelve tribes of Israel. Jesus chose twelve apostles. There are twelve signs of the zodiac."

"And for the Romans? Did it have a special significance?" Frost pressed.

Lili nodded. "It's possible. The Romans borrowed many of their religious ideas from other cultures. The Etruscans, for instance, established twelve major cities. The major Greek gods numbered twelve, and many of the Roman deities are patterned after the Greek pantheon. And as Tony said, there are twelve signs of the zodiac, which were also known to the Romans. When he became the dictator of Rome, Julius Caesar created a new calendar—it is the basis of the calendar we use today—dividing the year into twelve months. So yes, it's safe to assume twelve was significant."

Frost pushed at one of the carved sections, working the surface with his fingers. He found a soft spot and pressed a little harder and the crust around it crumbled, revealing a small hole about five centimetres in diameter. He worked a finger into the hole and felt some resistance. "Tony, hand me one of those spears."

Denison passed over the ancient relic, and Frost forced the butt-end into the hole he'd been working on. He experimented with it, first twisting the shaft in its socket like a key in a lock, and then pushed against it as though trying to wind a capstan.

Nothing happened.

But suddenly Lili was excited.

She pushed Frost aside, tugging the spear free. "You're right. You must be. We need to find the hole that corresponds with March."

Frost peered at the decorative carvings again, but saw nothing that resembled any sort of calendar symbols he'd ever seen, never mind letters or numbers.

Lili gazed at the centre stone for a moment. "Climb up there," she pointed to where the statue of Mars would have been.

Frost did as he was told, but he had no way of knowing how the missing statue would have originally been oriented. Lili seemed to. She directed him to turn to his right and then continued adjusting his position inch by inch until she was satisfied he was facing the same direction the statue would have been seventeen hundred years ago. "There. Don't move."

She circled around behind him and inserted the end of the spear into a hole that was at Frost's eight o'clock. As the shaft slid into the recess, there was a distinctive *click*. Frost heard it. They all did. He glanced over his shoulder and immediately saw the significance of what she had done. The spear jutted out from the circle in a perfect representation of the symbol of Mars. The sign of man.

Lili bent over the spear and began to push.

A grinding noise filled the chamber as the outer ring of the stone receptacle began to move. Denison rushed to Lili's side, and working together, they rotated the stone circle until the spear was pointing directly ahead of Frost.

He didn't move.

Something was happening.

He didn't want to break the magic, whatever it was.

As soon as the spear tip reached that position, there was a second, sharp *click*, and the pedestal beneath Frost's feet began to vibrate.

Before he could even think about jumping down to safety there was another sound: stones scraping and slamming together.

The centre circle, where he stood, and the outer perimeter of the pedestal didn't move, but the interior of the repository abruptly fell away into darkness.

FIFTEEN
LOW COUNTRY FOR OLD MEN

The Netherlands—0245 Local (0145 UTC)

Konstantin Khavin parked his hired car in a layby and got out, slamming the door behind him.

The night air, chilly from a sea breeze blowing across the lowlands, was cutting. The bite helped him shrug off the fatigue from the long train ride and subsequent drive through the flat Dutch countryside. To the south, he could make out the glow of the Hague-Rotterdam conurbation. The city was distant enough that he could see most of the landscape before him by starlight alone. He savoured the wind against his face a moment longer, and then turned his back on it. From now until the end of it, he was task-orientated. And the task was David Habersham.

He was less than two klicks from the front gate of Habersham's manor, but the property itself lay on the far side of the highway. Lethe's digging had tapped into the satellite feed and revealed there was no fence around the estate, and no evidence of security measures in place, which seemed odd for a man at the centre of an elaborate web of conspiracy theories and plots around the Crown. He had to assume the house itself was guarded.

Habersham was a powerful man, but not rich beyond dreams of avarice—a multi-millionaire, not a billionaire. Not Howard Hughes hiding behind impenetrable layers of security.

Or so Lethe thought; Konstantin wasn't so sure.

Walking a mile in Habersham's shoes, even with the loner mentality, if he'd been part of a terrorist conspiracy intent on fundamentally altering the world, he'd take every precaution guarding the approaches to his residence. Never think your enemy is an idiot or weaker than you. Never think he wouldn't do at least what you'd do, and at best would be three steps ahead of you, as he'd had forever to make contingencies.

With the aid of a Night Optics D-300 night vision monocular held to his eye by an uncomfortably jerry-rigged headband, he covered the ground quickly—moving through the tall grass as confidently as if it was bright daylight.

He scanned the area for motion sensors, security cameras, and any kind of hidden surveillance equipment. He stopped every few feet and listened with his eyes closed, straining to catch any sounds that didn't belong—anything out of the ordinary—anything that might herald the approach of a patrol. Silence. Ordinary night sounds.

Twenty-seven minutes after slamming the car door, he got his first glimpse of Habersham's house through a stand of Scots pine trees.

The house was a squat, single-story building with a gently sloping roof, built in the traditional colonial Dutch style. It was an utterly unremarkable place—not the home of a millionaire—save for the fact that at the north corner, it joined to the towering structure of an old-fashioned windmill, like something straight out of Cervantes, with enormous vanes turning slowly in the faint breeze.

Habersham had made his fortune from alternative energy production, so maybe the windmill was more than just an elaborate lawn ornament?

Despite the late hour, several of the windows in the house were lit from within.

Konstantin couldn't see any other signs of activity.

It took another hour's painstaking surveillance to satisfy the big Russian that there were no guards, no dogs, no cameras or sensors around the structure. That didn't make him happy, but he wasn't about to look a gift horse in the mouth. He broke from cover and crossed to the house, ducking behind the ponderous vanes of the windmill as they turned.

The mill's rustic appearance was a façade.

Up close, Konstantin could see that the vanes were made of metal, not wood—something lightweight and durable, and covered with a synthetic fabric. The axle around which the whole mechanism rotated was also of metal, and where it disappeared into the supporting structure, there was a metal gear box with traces of machine oil and grease seeping out around the spindle. The mill's windows were double-paned insulated glass set into vinyl frames; impossible to open from the outside, but the touch that was most at odds with the antiquated look of the mill was the door, which was equipped with a very modern push-button electronic lock.

Konstantin remained absolutely motionless for several minutes, to see if his approach had triggered any sensors on the lock box, or if he had been observed from the house itself. Then he took a closer look at the door.

The lock was a relatively unsophisticated affair, sporting a well-worn ten-digit keypad, nothing more elaborate than the kind of thing that would have been used to secure an office door in a shared building. It wouldn't take any particular skill to rig a fix for someone comfortable with electronic security. Konstantin was more of a hands-on, old-school kind of burglar though. He liked to listen to the movement of the tumblers in the locks, catch the subtle shift in sound as they dropped into place. There was an art to it. This modern stuff lacked sophistication. It was crass. It took the fun out of the game. You didn't need skill; you just needed a box of tricks. He wasn't averse to cheating.

But what it did mean was that getting into Habersham's house was going to be more difficult than breaking into Denison's flat had been.

He had come prepared.

He took a handheld electric circuit detector from the tool bag he'd brought along, and swept it around the doorframe. The lock registered immediately. There was no indication of other active circuits. The door wasn't alarmed.

He backed away from the door and tried to peer through the windows, but couldn't see anything inside because they were covered by heavy opaque curtains. That gave him pause. With the night vision scope, making a motion sensor would have been easy; now he was going to have to go in blind. He didn't like that. If there was an alarm system he'd have thirty to sixty seconds to disable it before everything went to hell.

He really hated technology.

The lock on the door was operated by an electromagnet; when the correct code was entered, the circuit would supply power to the magnet and pull back the bolt, permitting entry. Like most electronic security measures, the lock worked on the principle of a passive circuit. In order to make it work, you had to turn it on. Cutting power to the lock would merely leave the bolt in its locked position.

Konstantin didn't have the code, but he had something almost as good.

He delved into his bag of tricks again and took out a battery-operated degaussing gun. The handheld unit was nothing more than a very powerful electromagnet, used for erasing data from magnetic tape and computer disks. It was somewhere between old-school tech and the ultra-modern security breaker, and remarkably useful for a variety of not-so-legal applications.

He placed the degaussing magnet next to the doorknob and flipped the switch.

There was a metallic *click* from inside as the device grabbed hold of the spring-loaded bolt, magnetic attraction pulling it from the latch plate.

Konstantin sucked in a breath and then eased the door open.

It was as easy as that.

Inside the mill, all was quiet.

There was no warning tone of an active alarm system. No escalating cry of intruder, intruder to drown out his thoughts in panic and wake the dead. A sweep of the interior, one eye closed, so the night-vision monocle was the only image his brain had to process, didn't reveal anything either. No blinking indicator lights from concealed motion detectors or CCTV.

Something else stopped him in his tracks.

The interior room looked nothing at all like an old Dutch mill. There was no millstone grinding away patiently, no evidence at all in fact that the building served any sort of utilitarian purpose relating to the massive turbines outside.

The room was sparsely furnished: the only actual furniture was a single folding chair, positioned in the centre.

Directly in front of the chair was a camera tripod.

Right behind it, adorning the entire rear wall, was an enormous flag.

This didn't feel right.

He felt liked he'd stepped onto the set of a terrorist video circa 2001. He could imagine a man, face obscured by a scarf, leaning forward to lay claim to countless atrocities. He scanned the room. He couldn't determine the colour of the flag—it looked pure white in his night vision, but was probably some hue of red—but he had no difficulty making out the distinctive double-headed black eagle in the centre of the banner, positioned above a diagonal cross formed by the silhouettes of a scimitar and what was unmistakably a Kalashnikov assault rifle. The eagle was a common device in Eastern Europe, but it was the crossed weapons, along with the chair and the camera, that spoke volumes to the Russian.

This is a very bad place.

Something flashed at the edges of the monochrome display. Konstantin swivelled the monocle away. The light had come from outside. He moved quickly into the room and pulled the door shut behind him.

He paused in the darkness, just breathing, listening, and then opened the door a crack, looking to identify the source of the illumination.

To his unaided eyes, the spot of light was a barely-visible pinprick across nearly a kilometre of open terrain. As he continued to watch, the light divided like a pair of blazing eyes, drawing ominously closer: a vehicle approaching the house at speed.

He was about to have a visitor.

A white Volkswagen Eurovan emerged from the gloom and pulled to a stop in front the main house, thirty metres from where the Russian watched. As the driver and passenger got out, an older man emerged from the house to greet them. Konstantin recognised him from Lethe's dossier: David Habersham.

The driver of the van was dressed in black military fatigues, replete with a rolled up watch cap and a tactical vest. Konstantin noted the holstered pistol, and the compact Heckler & Koch MP-5 machine pistol slung from one shoulder.

The passenger was less remarkable.

He was of an age with Habersham, and had a thatch of silver-grey hair and a bottle-brush moustache. Light spilled out from the main house in a long rectangle across the driver. The man stepped into it, moving forward to greet Habersham. He wore a professorial tweed jacket, chinos, and rather nice shoes. There was no indication that he was armed; his jacket fell naturally as he pumped Habersham's hand.

Behind them, the driver slid open the van side door, revealing another uniformed man.

Habersham spoke first, his voice high with surprise and concern. It carried easily to where the Russian hid. "Where are the rest of your men? Was there a problem?"

"No problems." The man's accent was maddeningly familiar, but Konstantin couldn't place it. "Not here, at least. The operation went exactly as planned. The problem was elsewhere. My horseman needed some assistance."

"The sword?"

"It was not where we thought it would be, but the horseman is confident that it will be found. I sent the rest of my team to Rome to aide in its recovery. They should already be on the ground." The man clapped Habersham on the shoulder. "It is good to have a private jet, no?"

Habersham did not sound quite so sanguine. "Using the jet might arouse suspicion."

"No one will suspect anything. The trail will lead exactly where we wish it to."

Habersham shook his head slightly, doubting, obviously less than thrilled with the turn of events, and then approached the van.

He peered inside the rear cargo area.

After a moment, he drew back and addressed the H&K guy. "Put him in the mill."

Khavin's heart thudded in his chest.

He pulled the door shut quietly and retreated into the now totally dark interior.

He scanned the room again with the monocular. This time he made two doors against the back wall. One of them had a keyhole in the doorknob, the other did not.

Well that simplifies things.

Khavin went to the latter door and twisted the doorknob. Beyond was a stairwell—a utilitarian construct of steel and concrete—that ascended to the upper reaches of the mill. He went in, closing the door softly behind him.

He didn't go up.

Instead, he stayed there, his ear pressed to the door, trying to hear what was happening in the room he'd just left. If he was right about the room—about the chair and the flag and the camera—they wouldn't be going any further.

He waited. Time slowed.

After a long silence, Khavin heard the sharp *beep* of the exterior lock disengaging and a *thump* as someone threw the door wide open. There was a shuffling of feet and grunts of exertion, the drag of a chair leg on the stone floor, and then the room was quiet again.

Konstantin waited.

He listened, straining to catch the faintest whisper or creak of a floorboard, ready to exfiltrate via the stairs if any noises suggested he was about to be made.

Nothing.

And still he waited.

And still nothing.

Having completed their task, Habersham's men must have exited the mill.

Konstantin turned the latch and eased the door open a crack.

The room remained dark and still.

He pushed the door open another inch. It was enough to see the chair in the centre of the room.

It was occupied by a man, dressed in what looked like pyjamas.

He sat slumped in the chair, his arms bound behind his back, his head covered by a sack of dark cloth.

Habersham had taken a hostage.

Konstantin waited a moment longer to make sure that there wasn't a guard lurking in the darkness…

Of course there's not. A guard would turn on the lights.

…and then stole forward into the room.

The prisoner sat alone, unmoving and unaware of the Russian's presence. Konstantin continued to study the man through his night vision monocular, weighing up his options.

His original intention had been to gain access to Habersham's house, gather intel on the Four Evangelists and their plans. He still had no idea what their over-arching scheme entailed, but now he knew it involved this hostage, and that presented him with a dilemma: continue with his original plan, and risk learning the truth only after it was too late to abort? Or take definitive action—pre-emptive action—here and now, without knowing what was really going on?

But that wasn't really the choice before him.

He knew what awaited the prisoner.

The real choice came down to one question: was he prepared to let this man die?

He didn't know him.

He'd never met him

He didn't owe him anything.

So what was one life to him?

Konstantin Khavin smiled ruefully in the darkness. Not so many years ago, there would have been no dilemma. Who lived, who died, had been inconsequential then. Life had been cheap in the Soviet Union. Men and women were expendable. Pawns on the chessboard, sacrificed as needed for the sake of the mission and the glory of the Rodina.

His eventual defection was proof positive that he rejected such a mind-set.

He wasn't squeamish about death. He didn't for a moment imagine himself to be a selfless hero. He was no Shane riding into town to save the weak and the helpless. He was Konstantin Khavin: a man of beliefs that ran deeper and were more complex than humanity or religion. He wasn't a good man. Frost was a good man. Khavin was a hard man. He had it in him to be ruthless.

But even so, he could not shrug his shoulders and abandon this poor bastard to his fate.

There was no dilemma.

He moved close to the man in the chair, and then gently reached out and tugged off the head covering. The man started, panicking, kicking and struggling against his bonds, wild-eyed. He was petrified.

Konstantin took him to be in his sixties. Light-coloured hair—probably grey—and a thick moustache. He was on the stout side, and had a round, avuncular face, and jowls like ham hocks. In the green monochrome display of the night optics, his pupils were enormous white dots that seemed to stare right past the Russian without seeing him.

Konstantin tried to soothe him. "I'm a friend," he whispered in English.

"Who are you?"

A Slavic accent; the man wasn't a local. "A friend," he repeated. "I'm going to get you out of here, but if I am going to be able to do that, you're going to have to remain as quiet as possible. Understand?"

The man nodded.

Khavin didn't even think about questioning the man, even though learning his name might offer insight into Habersham's master plan. There would be time enough for that later. If they made it out of here.

He quickly cut the plastic zip-ties that bound the man's wrists together, and then helped him to his feet.

The older man was unsteady at first. He must have taken a blow to the head when they'd subdued him during the initial abduction. There was blood matted in his hair and scalp that showed up darkly in the monocular.

"Can you stand?"

He nodded.

Konstantin grasped the man's right hand and placed it on his own shoulder. "You'll be able to see better once we're outside," he whispered. "Until then, don't let go."

The man nodded again, and Konstantin immediately headed across the empty room to the door to the outside world.

Again, he eased it open a crack, listening, scanning the night for any hint of trouble ahead. The turbines creaked as they turned. There was no other movement. Very slowly, he opened the door wide.

A cool breeze swept over him, raising gooseflesh on the back of his neck.

His skin was damp with perspiration. He hadn't even realised he was sweating.

The air carried with it the scent of the fields, and a hint of something familiar...It was tobacco smoke. Someone was smoking a cigarette nearby, close enough that the breeze hadn't swept away the odour...Suddenly, something hard and heavy crashed into the side of his head, knocking the monocular away.

A fierce stab of pain lanced through his skull, followed by a flash of light.

And then his world went completely black.

SIXTEEN
THE TEMPLE

Rome—0318 Local (0218 UTC)

Denison directed the beam of his light down into the black void.

Frost saw that the bottom of the receptacle had dropped away in pieces, at graduated intervals, to form a staircase, spiralling around the pedestal. It mirrored the design of the staircase in the temple basin around them.

"Brilliant!" Denison was uncharacteristically giddy. Without any prompting, and before Frost could suggest caution, his friend had one leg over the low edge, and was lowering himself onto the stairs. With Lili close on his heels, he descended into the newly discovered passage, leaving Frost to bring up the rear once more.

He didn't like it.

He didn't like it one little bit.

Going deeper. More earth above his head. More ancient passageways.

Hesitantly, Frost stepped down from the plinth and followed them.

The twelve stone treads that had lowered were only the first part of a much longer stairway that coiled around a central pillar, dropping at least thirty metres. Frost descended carefully, making sure not to dislodge the spears of the *Salii* that still rested on the first eleven steps, and caught up to the others at the base of the staircase where it opened onto a balcony that ringed the interior of a vast, domed chamber.

"A subterranean Pantheon?" Denison exclaimed.

"There is a similarity," Lili agreed, excited. "Albeit on a smaller scale, and built at least a century before the time of Hadrian."

"No one has set foot in this room in centuries," Denison said.

Lili played her torch beam on the walls, illuminating pillars and arches of smooth grey. "This is concrete, not carved stone."

"So it's new, then?" Frost asked.

She shook her head. "The Romans discovered the secret of making concrete in ancient times. They utilized it extensively in the construction of bridges and aqueducts, and of course, the many temples and other buildings that still stand today. The knowledge was lost during the Dark Ages, and only rediscovered in more recent times."

She turned her light onto the darkness below.

A single piece of statuary rested on a pedestal in the exact centre of the chamber: a life-sized figure of a sitting man. His face was handsome and commanding beneath a skull bald save for a fringe of curly hair. It wasn't stone. It was some kind of dark metal. *Bronze*, Frost guessed. There was something resting on its lap that glinted back brightly in the torchlight. Rich. Warm. Gold. Like the sun trapped in the centre of the earth.

"That's Caesar," Lili said, breathlessly. "Even before his death, he was deified—a living god. This place is a temple to Julius Caesar."

Frost knew what was coming next.

"And that's the sword," Denison said, fixing his beam on the statue's knees. The weapon that lay across them was, unmistakably, an unsheathed Roman *gladius*.

The brass hilt gleamed like gold. There was no crosspiece or any kind of hand guard, save for the shape of the hilt itself, which flared out a little where it wrapped around the blade. That blade was half-a-metre long, perfectly straight, except at the tip, where it angled to a severe point, and miraculously untarnished by oxidation. Despite the passage of two millennia the steel seemed mirror bright, as if it had been polished just yesterday.

As Denison played his light along its length, the reflection danced like yellow flame.

He let the light linger there only a moment before turning away and hastening around the balcony to another staircase that led down the floor of the temple.

Lili was moving almost as quickly.

They were halfway to the statue before Frost said, "Stop!"

Denison stopped in his tracks and turned to look up at him, his face a mixture of irritation and concern.

"Use your head," Frost called down to them. "This place was built for the sole purpose of protecting that sword. Secret passages inside secret rooms. They didn't just leave it here unprotected."

When he received only blank looks, Frost drove the point home. "Am I the only one who's ever watched Indiana bloody Jones?"

Denison cocked an eyebrow in Lili's direction.

"He's right. The Romans were exceptional engineers. Touch nothing. Not until we know it is safe."

Denison nodded and played his light around the otherwise empty chamber. "What are we looking for, then? Some sort of mechanism?"

Lili scanned the room, following his torch with her eyes as the beam fell on the feet of the statue directly in front of them. "They worshipped at Caesar's feet," she mused. "If there is a trap, it would be designed to prevent anyone from removing the sword, not prevent worship."

She resumed walking, more cautiously now, until the huge sculpture was less than an arm's length away. "Here," she pointed. "There is a seam where the pedestal meets the floor. Those stairs back there utilised some kind of counterweight mechanism. It could be the same principle here... some kind of balancing mechanism below us. Removing the sword might upset the balance."

"That would make sense," Denison agreed.

"So if we remove it, we need to put something else there of equal weight, or just heavy enough to hold it down?"

Lili frowned. "Impossible to know."

Frost was reminded vividly of every soldier's nightmare: stepping on a live landmine, hearing that *click* as the pressure sensitive mechanism was armed, and knowing that no matter how fast you ran, no matter what you did, the mine would detonate the instant your foot came off the trigger. There were methods for fooling a mine, of course. It could even be disarmed *in situ*, but the odds of surviving were not good. Once the mine was armed, the slightest change in pressure could cause it to blow.

They weren't literally standing on a live landmine, but they might as well be.

And Denison and Lili weren't going to leave without the sword.

So, how do I beat this landmine?

"I've got an idea," Frost said, thinking on his feet.

He darted back up the spiral staircase and then returned, bearing several of the ceremonial spears in his arms.

"That won't work," Lili said, misreading his intent. "If the sword weighs more or less than a spear by even a few grams, it might upset the balance."

Frost shook his head. "Not where I was going. We can jam the spear points into the seam at the base of the pedestal... wedge it in place."

"And keep it from moving when we remove the sword," Denison finished for him. "The mechanism can't be too sensitive. They have earthquakes here, remember?"

Indeed, the northern Emilia-Romagna region had experienced a recent spate of devastating quakes over the last few years that had led some fundamentalist Christians to believe it was God's judgment against the Church for centuries of misrule.

"If we're careful, and lucky, the statue won't move a millimetre," Frost promised as he handed one of the spears to Denison.

A closer examination verified Lili's first suspicion.

Not only was there a discernible gap between the pedestal and the floor, but a firm but gentle sideways pressure on the statue caused that gap to widen perceptibly, and relieving that pressure allowed it to ease back into place, as though the pedestal were a boat bobbing next to a jetty. This only heightened Frost's anxiety about what he was about to do.

He glanced at Lili. "Maybe you should take a step back."

She shook her head.

He shrugged, and then ever so gently, worked the tip of a spear into the black seam, being careful not to push it too deep. He kept the pressure on the spear steady as he managed to work it in a full centimetre in, and saw the gap widen a little to accommodate it as the metal point went deeper still. Finally, he backed away, leaving the shaft protruding upright from the floor.

Denison gave a nod of satisfaction and began trying to work his spear into the joint on the opposite side.

"Well that's fortunate," he said after a moment, but he didn't sound all that happy with his fortune. "It's wedged tight. I couldn't even force the tip in—and I haven't said that since my wedding night." It wasn't the best joke, but Lili offered a grudging smile. "Let's put it to the test then, shall we?" He sucked in a breath and wrapped the fingers of his right hand around the bright brass hilt of the Crocea Mors.

After another pause and another breath, he lifted the ancient sword from its resting place.

Nothing happened.

No deadly trap sprung closed.

Frost realised he had been holding his breath.

He let it out with a sigh.

"Right. That's it then. Mission well and truly accomplished. We have the sword, so let's get the hell out of here."

They ignored him.

Denison held the sword up in awe. "The sword of Julius Caesar," he whispered. "The sword of kings. I never imagined I would hold it."

Lili took a step toward him and reached out as though intending to take her turn marvelling in their discovery, but before he handed it over she let her hand fall. "The Irishman is right. We are not safe here. We must go."

Denison nodded absently and backed away from the statue, but his mind was clearly elsewhere. He continued to hold the sword out reverently, but something about his stance worried Frost. It seemed as though he were poised for combat.

He'd taken only three steps away from the statue when a low keening sound began to reverberate through the chamber, growing in intensity as it echoed back and forth from the sides of dome.

"What the—?"

A loud clang momentarily broke through the hum, and Frost saw that Denison had dropped the sword and was staring at it wide-eyed in disbelief. He glanced at his companions then pointed at the antique weapon on the concrete floor. "It's not me... I didn't do anything. The sword..." He had to shout to be heard over the escalating hum. "It started to vibrate in my hands."

Frost was still processing his claim when a new sound cut through the resonance waves—the scraping of stone. It took him a moment to place it: up above. There was another sound, metal hitting stone.

Frost glimpsed the shaft of the spear he'd wedged into the side of the pedestal as it clattered to the floor, its point no longer holding the statue in place.

"Shit," he rasped, instinctively turning for the stairs.

Lili moved too, but instead of seeking the exit, she darted back and scooped the sword from the dusty floor.

She grabbed Denison's hand in her own and dragged him into motion.

A new sound joined the tumult. It was more than just noise. Frost felt the vibration in the soles of his feet like the beginning of an earthquake.

But it was no earthquake.

With a sound like a gunshot, a section of the wall on the far side of the chamber exploded outward, driven by an immense pressure-jet of water. Two more sections of wall were blasted away, giant stones shattering as they impacted, propelled by an unrelenting torrent of water. In a matter of seconds, the entire floor of the domed chamber was a foot underwater, and the flow from the three spouts showed no sign of slowing.

"So much for being clever. *Go*," Frost yelled, splashing toward the stairs.

By the time he put his first foot on the stone steps the ice-cold water was well over his knees and getting deeper fast.

From the balcony, the situation looked no less dire.

The water was rising fast—it was already lapping at the feet of the bronze Caesar. Frost started to climb the spiral stair. As he did, he saw that the ancient Roman guardians of the sword had anticipated exactly this: the final twelve steps of the stairway had risen back into their original position and the aperture that would have led them out had slammed shut.

He swallowed down the urge to scream out his frustration: right now he needed his wits about him. He could panic about drowning down here later. *Better than being buried alive*, he thought mawkishly. *But not much.*

Frost played his light overhead, looking for a weakness, a chink, anything he could exploit. The torch beam lit the underside of the stone circle. From this angle, he could see the ropes and pulleys that connected the steps to the mechanism in the spear receptacle, and he could see that one of the ancient ropes had broken, leaving one of the twelve steps in its lowered position. It wasn't much. But it was a start. The step was almost waist high. The water hadn't reached it yet. More importantly, he hoped, there was a gap in the ceiling where the aperture hadn't closed flush. There was no guarantee he'd be able to wriggle through it, but if he could get to the step, and climb using the recesses where the steps should have been, maybe he could get them out of here.

"See that?" Frost speared his light up at the gap above them, and then at the lone step, and traced the six black holes that rose up around the curve of the wall. "Think you can make it?"

He didn't wait for an answer, but crouched in place and then leaped out across the gap, slamming into the wall and very nearly staggering back into the rising water. He spread himself wide, feeling out the hand holds one at a time, and with his saturated clothes weighing heavily on him, started the hand over hand climb until he reached a point where he could use his feet to brace himself. His soaking jeans had left a wet trail along the wall. It was only going to get worse as the others followed him. With Denison coming last it was going to be treacherous. He would have been last, but with his arm, he wasn't sure he'd have been able to make it. Sometimes you couldn't afford to be a gent.

"Lili! Your turn," he called back. "Follow me."

He expected her to balk, but her hesitancy had nothing to do with the thought of leaping out into space. To his dismay, he saw her eyes drop to the sword she still clutched in her right hand.

"Leave it," Frost urged. "It's not worth dying for."

Water was flooding into the stairwell now; soon it would reach the lowest of the hand holds, and the step would be gone. The subterranean chamber was filling up much faster than he would have believed possible. It must have been half of the Tiber emptying into the chamber. There wasn't a second to waste worrying about the fate of a bloody sword.

"If you don't jump now, you'll die here with it. We know where it is. We can come back."

But Lili ignored him.

Instead of surrendering the blade to an uncertain fate, she carefully threaded it into her belt, and only when it was secure did she gather herself for the jump.

Shaking his head at her sheer bloody obstinacy, Frost worked himself around the angle to give her more room. She was athletic. Lithe. But she wasn't a long jumper. She didn't make it. Her foot caught the edge of the stone step. She tried to adjust but couldn't, and fell forward, the side of her head hitting the wall as she lunged only to fall back. She hit the rising water and went under, and Frost knew he didn't have a choice. He launched himself from a height, spearing down into the water, kicking and splashing as it rose relentlessly, and swam across to where she was floating face down, like a starfish, bleeding.

He turned her in his arms, tilting her head so she wasn't swallowing water, and trod water while it rose around them. He couldn't climb with her in his arms and he couldn't leave her behind.

He looked at Denison. "Go. Get that fucking thing open, or we're all dead."

Denison didn't hesitate.

He took a few steps back to get a running start, and then jumped easily across the gap, then climbed hand-over-hand with a surety that belied his age.

Soon he was up by the aperture, and trying to get some sort of purchase on it to force the gap wider. The mechanisms grated back on themselves, the sound lost in the sheer tumult of churning water flooding the chamber, but the aperture was visibly wider.

Denison looked back down at him, nodded once, and then kicked off the side and scrabbled upwards, pulling himself through the aperture.

He was swallowed by the darkness.

Now all Frost could do was wait for the chamber to flood and the water carry him toward the aperture.

Lili kicked out, struggling suddenly, and nearly dragging him down.

"Relax," Frost said, "I've got you. You're safe. Stop struggling." But she wouldn't. She fought him, and her struggles dragged them down.

Frost swallowed a huge lungful of water.

All he could see was black water.

There was nothing else.

Lili thrashed, splashing, and pulled away from him.

He pushed for the surface but his jeans snagged on the head of Caesar, keeping him under. Frost thrashed in panic, kicking out, wriggling and writhing and twisting trying to tear it free, and then he was loose and rising.

When he broke the surface he saw Denison reaching down through the aperture to help Lili up.

His heart was hammering in his chest.

For a moment—just a moment, a single sickening fraction of a second—he'd thought he was going to die, and thought Lili had done it deliberately, betraying them for the sword.

Gulping down a breath of stale foetid air, he could hardly breathe a sigh of relief, but he was so, so glad to be wrong.

She disappeared up into the darkness.

Frost trod water, gazing up, waiting for Denison to reappear with his helping hand. The water rose mercilessly. Time was lost in the surge and churn and splash of water, and then the jets were under the surface, making a brutal battering undertow that threatened to drag him under. "In your own time, mate!" He yelled up at the hole above him.

When the other man finally reappeared, it wasn't to lend a helping hand.

Denison plummeted through the opening, crashing onto Frost before he could even think about trying to swim out of the way, and both men were dragged under.

SEVENTEEN
BEACON

Rome—0327 Local (0227 UTC)

The impact of Denison's fall coupled with the sheer power of the jets pumping water mercilessly into the chamber dragged Frost down. There was nothing he could do to fight it. Water buffeted and battered him from all sides, twisting him as he tried to claw his way back to the surface.

His light was gone, his and Denison's. The dark left him disoriented. He knew he had to fight his way back to the surface and just wait it out as the water rose.

And pray they didn't seal the aperture before he did.

He reached out, desperately trying to grab on to anything solid. His fingers closed on something soft and yielding instead. "Tony?" He called out. The darkness swallowed his words. It was a body. It had to be him.

He pulled Denison close, lifting his head above the surface.

He was breathing. Thank god. He hooked his arm under and around Denison and held his head above the water until Denison broke into a fit of coughing.

"Tony?" Frost's teeth chattered. He clenched them. The cold gnawed away at him as he trod water. The exertion of keeping them both up coupled with freezing cold made each word an ordeal. "What the hell happened?"

"Waiting for us," Denison managed between shivering and choking. "They took Lili...they...took the *sword*."

"It's just a sword. We've got to get out of here." He tried to process with it meant: Denison's enemies had found them, had followed them into the hidden passages and lain in wait. Something about that didn't feel right; it nagged away at Frost, and wouldn't let go. But the urgency of their current predicament had to take precedence. "There's got to be another way out of here," he shouted above the pouring water. Whitecaps frothed around them from the churning undercurrents.

A light flared suddenly as Denison reached with one hand up out of the water. The MagLite was waterproof. It was the first bit of luck they'd had in ages.

Frost saw the aperture, still open. The water had risen nearly a metre since Denison's fall. If the aperture stayed open they would be able to pull themselves through it as easily as climbing out of a swimming pool.

Assuming there's no one waiting up there to put a bullet in our heads as soon as we appear.

The chill sapped his strength by degrees. His clothes and shoes were like cement weights dragging him down. He had to battle for every breath, but he had trained for situations like this, facing cold and mounting exhaustion. He could shut off part of his brain and just survive. The ache in his arm was a bitch, but the one good thing about the cold water was his entire body had long since gone numb. Yet that numbness could still prove to be a killer: he couldn't seem to stay above the surface long enough to draw more than a breath or two, before the cold clamped his chest and he started to sink again.

He couldn't seem to get enough air to maintain buoyancy.

And then, like a light at the end of an impossibly long tunnel, the aperture was only a few feet above the still-rising water.

With an all-out effort, he kicked hard and propelled himself up, reaching for the lip of the aperture to haul himself up over the top. He struggled to support his own weight and would have fallen back into the water if Denison hadn't swum beneath him and braced his kicking legs. He made it over the top and rolled onto his back, shivering, panting, and otherwise motionless.

The killers were gone.

They'd been targeting Denison—at least that had been his assumption. But if that was the case, why they had taken Lili? Why had they pushed Denison back through the aperture, rather than put a bullet in his head?

He was missing something important.

He wasn't thinking clearly.

All that mattered to him now was getting out of this place.

Denison dragged himself up. They were back in the *sacellum*—the chamber where a modern priesthood still conducted rituals to honour the Roman god of war.

And there was only one way out of this place that he knew of: back the way they'd come.

"Any other way out of here than the Path of Mars? I'd rather not go back that way, in case they're expecting us."

Denison shook his head. "Unlikely."

"Great."

The two men didn't speak after that. They shuffled toward the exit, willing their hypothermic legs into a jog. Denison's light was inadequate. They moved mainly on memory.

Then they reached an intersection.

Frost stared at the crossroads in consternation. Lili had effortlessly guided them through the maze of passages, with a familiarity that he had found troubling. He'd paid attention to their route but even so, it was suddenly difficult to be sure which way they'd come, and this was only the first of a dozen such crossings.

"I think we went straight through," Denison said, without conviction.

Frost nodded and they started moving again, but at a more subdued pace.

And that was the only thing that saved their lives.

Seven steps up the passage, the floor abruptly vanished beneath Denison's feet.

The entire section of floor, at least twenty metres long, had tilted as soon as Denison stepped onto it. One end angled down steeply with his added weight, while the other end rose sharply, like a playground seesaw.

Frost lunged forward and grasped ahold of one of Denison's pin-wheeling arms as he desperately struggled to catch his balance. Frost hauled him from the pitfall trap. The pivoting section rose and fell, back and forth, slowly balancing again to its original state.

"I told you guys, Indiana bloody Jones," Frost shook his head.

"I don't think we came this way," Denison remarked wryly.

Frost just nodded. He understood now why Lili had been so quick to accept the possibility that the ancients had utilized a booby trap to protect the Crocea Mors; she must have known about other traps in the underground complex—meaning this was the first of many.

"We backtrack," he said. "Process of elimination."

Denison agreed, "It's not like we have a choice."

They retraced their steps to the junction and took the right-hand passage, walking slowly now and testing every step of the passage ahead. There were no obvious traps or mechanisms, but this was of little comfort. The purpose of the maze was two-fold: to disorient a would-be intruder, and protect the Path of Mars, meaning there would be only one correct path, and potentially dozens of false trails that ended in death. In the distance he could hear the churning water.

He remembered seeing the water table marks and realised that eventually, the entire Path of Mars would be flooded out.

That didn't help his mood.

They arrived at another junction. This time they methodically chose the right hand passage, but after a few steps, Frost noticed that the walls and ceilings were perforated with dozens of holes, each large enough for a spear to be thrust through. He assumed that a few steps on, they'd hit a pressure switch that would release spring-loaded spikes. They retreated, taking another path. And then another. And another. Thoroughly turning themselves around and around again.

There was nothing they could do about it. They had to explore one section of the labyrinth after another, and the time ticked mercilessly on. Frost noticed the film of water on the ground beneath their feet. They splashed on. It would still be hours until the entire subterranean network flooded. Sometimes a tunnel led them into traps; sometimes it took the pair to dead ends and forced them to retreat.

They did not speak, except as it related to their immediate need, and the silence was every bit as oppressive as the threat of the deadly pitfalls and spear-traps.

Then, with no real sense of having made any progress, they arrived at a stairwell leading up.

Frost looked at Denison.

"This is it," Denison said, visibly relieved. "Let's make like a shepherd."

"And get the flock out of here," Frost finished for him.

Frost ascended cautiously. There was always the possibility that Denison was wrong, and the Romans had left one last kick in the nuts for any intruders clever enough to get this far. There was always the potential for ambush, too.

However, the stairs did look familiar.

As he reached the top, he saw the gouges and scrapes on the floor where the loose section of the pilaster had been moved to alternately open or seal the entrance to the Path of Mars.

The men who'd taken Lili had dragged the block back into its original place, shutting the door. "Give me the torch," he told Denison, and played the light around the seams, looking for any chinks or fissures they could get ahold of from this side. There were four very basic handholds carved into the block. Together, they worked it open inch by inch until fresh air—warm and humid—washed over them.

Frost saw the purple hue of pre-dawn twilight overhead.

They had made it.

There was no obvious ambush waiting for them. He scanned the area before stepping out: no sign of anyone at all. Even so, they stayed in the shadows as they crept out of the Mausoleum of Augustus and made their way back to the waiting car.

Denison sank wearily into the passenger seat and rubbed the bridge of his nose. He'd aged twenty years overnight. "I'm sorry, Frosty. I don't know what comes next. They beat us."

Frost regarded his old friend.

You're on the wrong side...

He didn't want to believe it.

He didn't even know what the sides were.

But beyond the simple fact that they had been hunted—tracked halfway across Europe—there were other pieces of the puzzle that just didn't fit, no matter how he looked at it. Not the least of which was the fact that somehow, he'd been cut off from Nonesuch.

"Okay, mate; something's not right about this."

"I don't follow you."

"We've missed something."

"No we haven't. We had the sword. We lost it. We lost Lili. What's to miss?"

"These guys—these agents of the evil New Order, or whatever you called them—were after *you*, Tone." He stabbed a finger into Denison's chest to emphasize the point. "Kill Tony Denison: that was their only objective, right? So riddle me this: why did they take Lili? And why, after all the trouble it took to track you down in an entirely different country, didn't they kill you when they had the chance?"

Denison blinked at him. "I don't—"

"I don't either, but I'm beginning to think you were wrong about them, what they wanted... fuck, even *who* they really are."

"I..." The other man shook his head.

"Because I feel like I've been sold a dummy." Frost started the car. "One thing's for sure: we can't do anything to help Lili, or ourselves, until we know what's really going on."

He didn't elaborate on how he intended to bridge the knowledge gap because, in truth, he didn't know.

As he threaded the Fiat through the unfamiliar streets, searching for a main thoroughfare, he spotted a battered phone box on the side of the road. Something approaching inspiration dawned. He wasn't fluent in Italian, but that didn't stop him from finding what he was looking for in the ratty directory that hung from a chain beneath the phone: a listing for a twenty-four-hour cybercafé. He cross-referenced the address against the torn pages of map in the back of the directory. If he was right, it was only a few streets away. He tore the map out of the phone book and clambered back into the car.

The next time he stopped, Frost parked on the northern edge of a triangular *piazza* near the cybercafé. The piazza was dominated by an incredibly elaborate fountain, rendered in travertine, depicting a merman—*Neptune*, Frost supposed—resting on the upraised tails of four dolphins. Water spat from a conch shell. It was familiar, even though he'd never seen it before. That wasn't surprising, though, given the worldwide obsession with the artwork and sculptures of the Eternal City post-Dan Brown. There were puzzles and secrets in all of them, if the thriller writer was to be believed. *Lili would know what it is*, he thought.

The cybercafé was nearly empty; unsurprising, given the hour. But the clerk spoke decent English, and didn't seem to care about their bedraggled state. Given the fact the rear wall of the place was filled with seedy porn magazines and little index cards and tear-off adverts on a cork noticeboard, it was hardly surprising. The clerk passed over a slip of paper with their temporary access code. Frost nodded his thanks.

He found a terminal which allowed him to keep his back to the wall and offered a view of the door and the plate glass window, while keeping him away from the handful of other patrons. He sat and fired up the machine.

Denison, who had scarcely spoken a word in the last half-an-hour, sank into a nearby chair. He looked like a man who'd lost everything.

Rather than being annoyed and wanting to kick his arse into shape, Frost was grateful for his old mate's pessimistic turn; the last thing he needed right now was Denison looking over his shoulder.

He started by immediately trying to log into the Ogmios intranet, but hit an 'unauthorised access' warning. The bounce amplified the sense of dread he'd felt since Saint Albans.

The wrong side... He was still trying to work out how his decision to help Denison could've blown back so hard and so fast onto Nonesuch, but there was no getting away from the fact that the gunman on Holywell Hill had known exactly who he was. That presented two likely alternatives: either Ogmios had also been targeted, or Sir Charles had chosen to disavow him. Everything they did was deniable.

No, *he thought.* The old bastard wouldn't do that.

But another voice in his head kept whispering: *You're on the wrong side of this.*

He tried his personal, unsecured email account—nothing of interest there, unless he was thinking about prescription meds, penis enhancement and cheap auto-insurance. Then, checking his reflection in the security mirror in the corner to ensure Denison wasn't looking, he tapped a request into the search engine:

Anthony Denison

There was a momentary pause as the search went out onto the worldwide web, and then something extraordinary happened.

A list of the top ten hits appeared on the monitor screen, but instead of the scattershot of information Frost had expected—links to Denison's books, discussions about his polarised political opinions, even connections to other men who shared his name—he saw a none-too-subtle accusation:

The Four Evangelists
Is former Brigadier Anthony Denison part of the nationalist conspiracy known as the Four Evangelists? Find out more by clicking here.

It wasn't the content of the linked website that raised the hairs on the nape of Frost's neck, but rather the fact that every single one of the hits returned directed him to the same website. Search engines didn't work like that, meaning someone had messed with the code to make sure that anyone asking about Tony Denison would find their way to this particular website. There was only one person Frost could think of who'd do such a thing.

"Lethe," he whispered.

Unable to make contact through conventional means, Jude Lethe had built a digital bonfire to get his attention.

So what the hell are the Four Evangelists?

His eyes darted across the text, trying to work out what Lethe was trying to tell him.

The page contained a hasty description of a quasi-religious terrorist group intent on reshaping the world. It was short on detail, but the second paragraph gave a list of possible members—a list that started with Denison—along with their occupations.

Frost read on, swallowing the information in huge, undigested chunks. It didn't take a great leap to see how it all fit together with what Denison was doing. More importantly, it explained why the man had been targeted.

The last paragraph listed contact information, a phone number, which Frost committed to memory.

He sat back in his chair.

The wrong side... I'm still missing something.

He scanned the list of suspected members of the Four Evangelists. One other name stood out. He opened another window and typed in a new query. This time, the search performed as expected, and a few clicks later, he had found the verification he was looking for. Now it all made sense.

"Tony."

Denison raised his head.

"Tell me about the Four Evangelists."

The other man stiffened. "Where did you—?"

Frost silenced him. "No more games."

Denison shook his head. Frost saw the way his hand curled around the grip of his chair's armrest. He blinked once, twice, three times, four, as though his eyes were an indicator of his mental processing speed.

"I'm waiting," Frost said.

Finally, he took a breath and started speaking. "The Four Evangelists..."

Frost fought back a rising wave of anger. "Talk." He'd never completely bought into Denison's conspiracy theory, but now he knew for sure the other man had been holding back critical information, and that it had nearly gotten them killed. There was no friendly smile now. No for-old-times-sake.

"What I told you about the New World Order is the absolute truth. I haven't lied to you, Ronan. They're the greatest threat our society has ever faced. If they get their way, it will mean a return to serfdom without end. No more nations, no more superpowers. No more United Kingdom, just billions of people permanently enslaved to the multinational corporations and banks that own everything."

"Jesus Christ, Tony, have you heard yourself? You're worse than Tom fucking Cruise."

He took a breath, trying to rein in his passion. "Some of us have been shouting the message in the streets for a long time, but no one seems to care. But there are others who are ready to take action. That's what the Four Evangelists are.

"For the longest time, I thought they were just another crazy conspiracy rumour." He flashed a self-deprecating smile and for a moment—just a moment—seemed to come alive again. "There are a lot of loonies out there, Frosty, and they'll believe anything.

"In the Book of Revelation, four creatures bear witness to the coming of the Kingdom of God. They're sometimes called the 'Four Evangelists.' Do you know what that word means? 'Messengers of good news,' and that's what they are."

Frost remained impassive as the other man began describing the theory, proposed by a prominent Italian Bible scholar—the very man whose name Frost had earlier picked out from the list—that the Revelation had been a blueprint for overthrowing Rome, and not a prophecy of the end of days. Everything Denison said was virtually identical to what Frost had read on Lethe's website, but he got the sense that the other man was hedging, not tipping his hand.

"What's the plan? There's got to be a plan. Revelation was a blueprint, a strategy. Explain what you mean by that? And then tell me what the fuck this has got to do with Caesar's sword."

"The Four make their first appearance in Revelation, chapter four. But it's later, in chapter six, when they actually begin to speak. Each one of them bears witness to the arrival of a horse with a rider—"

"The Four Horsemen of the Apocalypse," Frost said.

Denison nodded. "Even people who don't know anything about the Bible have heard of the Four Horsemen. They're iconic. They're as recognizable as McDonald's golden arches, but the thing is, no one can agree on exactly what they represent. And the interpretation changes with every generation. But according to Professor Martedi, the horsemen were never meant to be a prophecy of something to come, but rather a description of a four-pronged strategy that would bring the Roman Empire to its knees. Four separate elements set up like dominoes, which would shake the power of Rome. The first—the white horseman—is described as wearing a crown and carrying a bow. In the first century, that represented the emergence of a strong Parthian king. The second horse—a red horse, whose rider carries a great sword—represented a state of total war. The third horseman carried scales and was associated with both famine and rising food prices. The fourth horse represented death by every means, but is especially linked to pestilence.

"A great nation can withstand a crisis—a war, an economic downturn—but when the crises multiply, arriving one atop another, the foundation crumbles. In the first century, the plan was never fully executed, and Rome endured, but the wisdom of the strategy holds true even today."

"Treat me like an idiot, spell it out for me," Frost pressed. "Who are the horsemen?"

Denison balked at the directness of the question. "I—I don't know. I'm not part of this, Ronan. I don't know the details. I'm not even sure the horsemen are meant to identify literal people.

"But think about it. A strong leader emerges, someone charismatic who can rally people when everything looks hopeless. At the same time, war, economic hardship, perhaps even a disease pandemic like AIDS or Bird Flu, something like that, and you throw the forces of globalism into chaos. It's already started. Look at what more than a decade of war has done to the United States. Look at what's happening in the Eurozone. Greece on the verge of ruin, Spain and Ireland in trouble. The Euro currency itself under threat. And experts say we're overdue for some kind of plague outbreak. When all of these forces finally collide, it will rip our world to shreds."

"And that's when your white horse will ride in and rescue everyone?" Frost couldn't entirely mask the sarcasm in his tone. "That's why you wanted to find Caesar's sword, isn't it? The Arthurian Myth. Excalibur, the Once and Future King and all that. It's a symbol of the Divine Right of Kings, a way to seal the deal."

Denison inclined his head. "A symbol, yes. One that would affirm the Crown in the hearts and minds of the subjects once more."

Frost shook his head. "You're smarter than this, Tony. You said it yourself. These men don't see Revelation as a prophecy... they aren't waiting for these things to happen. It's a strategy, and they want to implement it. They want to make it happen. Start the next world war, rip the world economy apart, unleash bird flu or smallpox or some designer fucking virus there's no cure for. That's not visionary, Tony. It's insanity."

Denison ducked his head, unable to meet Ronan's eye.

"What about Lili?"

The question caught the former brigadier off guard. "Lili?"

"She's in on this too, isn't she?"

This time it was Denison's turn to shake his head. "Lili's an historian. She's been helping me track down the sword. Nothing more."

Frost could almost see the cogs turning inside Denison's head, the cogs driving the shafts that turned the wheels, and he knew the man was looking at Lili's role in a new light. "Damn it, Tony, you can't be that naïve. How did you two connect? Why were you working with her? No secrets. We're in deep shit here. I need to know the truth."

"David Habersham suggested it."

Frost recognised the name from the list on the website. "Habersham? He *is* one of the Four."

Denison nodded slowly. "He wants the same thing I do: the full restoration of the monarchy. I guess that would make him the first of the Four: the one who announces the rider on the white horse. He knew of my passion for Arthurian lore, and was aware of my acquaintance with Lili's father. When he learned about her discovery of the palimpsest, he suggested that we meet. Believe me, Ronan; David is a very influential man. He even arranged for me to meet with... ah, my patron."

"Your patron," Frost echoed. "The man who would be king?"

The haunted look in Denison's eyes was answer enough.

"What the fuck have you gotten yourself into, Tony? Habersham put you and Lili together, pulled the strings for you to serve the man who would be king. You don't think any of this is the least bit suspicious?"

Denison spread his hands in a helpless gesture.

It was true after all; he *was* on the wrong side.

But was there really even a right side?

"We have to stop them. You understand that, don't you? I don't care how much you believe in what they're doing, we can't let them unleash this on the world. Not *any* of it."

Denison didn't answer, didn't meet his gaze.

Frost rubbed his eyes wearily.

He understood almost everything now. He understood why Denison had been marked for death; he understood who the real enemy was, and what he would have to do to stop them.

There was only one thing that still troubled him.

"Back there in the crypt, when you picked up the sword, what happened?"

Denison abruptly sat up in his chair, his eyes coming alive at the memory.

"It was incredible," he said. "I don't know how to explain it. I really don't. I felt it in every bone in my body." And then the front of Tony Denison's face exploded as a 7.62×51mm NATO round tore out of it.

The exit wound left nothing recognisable behind.

EIGHTEEN
Q & A

Location unknown—0345 UTC (approximate)

A dull, insistent, thump of pain brought Konstantin Khavin back slowly to consciousness.

It took him a moment to realise it wasn't from the blow that had taken him down—though he felt a knot growing at the back of his skull from that hit.

The dull ache was amplified by pressure change. The pain pulsed in time with his heartbeat.

I'm on an aircraft, he realised.

Konstantin opened his eyes.

He saw nothing.

There was something covering his face—a hessian sack. He twisted, trying to move, to dislodge the sack, but it just twisted with his head. As his awareness sharpened, he felt the heavy fabric against his skin and tasted the stale air that he had been breathing over and over again.

He worked his jaw, wincing as the movement aggravated his injury.

He was rewarded with a not altogether pleasant *pop* in his inner ear as the pressure equalised. That small measure of relief freed him to begin piecing together what had happened.

The last thing he remembered clearly was freeing Habersham's hostage.

Though he hadn't actually freed him.

At least they hadn't just killed him outright, which is what he would have done in their place. Given the set up at Habersham's mill—the camera positioned facing the militant flag, the chair in the middle of the bare concrete floor—he wondered if a quick death might have been preferable.

He was seated with his hands bound behind his back, the nylon cat-strangler ties biting into his wrists and ankles. The heavy bag over his head blocked out light and amplified the noise of his own laboured breathing, but when he held his breath for a moment, he could just make out the sound of muffled voices nearby.

"—should postpone. Or reconsider altogether."

Habersham.

"You're being paranoid." A stern rebuke. The voice belonged to the man that had brought the hostage to Habersham's manor house. Those three words proved that he was at least Haberhsam's equal in the group. Another evangelist? Or was there one above them? A messianic leader?

"Paranoid? I rather think not. There are questions we should be asking: who is he? How did he find us? If someone on the outside knows what we're doing, then we've already lost."

"Then let's wake him up and ask him."

There was a pause, and then something collided with the side of Konstantin's head. The blow set his ears ringing and triggered a concomitant stab of pain at the base of his skull.

"Wake up," the second man growled in his ear.

Konstantin gritted his teeth and turned his head to indicate that he had heard.

"Who are you, my friend? Who do you work for?"

Konstantin knew intuitively that these men were amateurs. They learned their tradecraft from watching Jack Bauer and Jason Bourne use brute force to solve all their problems. Konstantin smiled beneath his hood, and then spat an oath in his native tongue.

"What's that?" Habersham immediately asked. "Russian? Is he a KGB agent?"

The other man spoke into his ear. "The KGB haven't existed for twenty years, have they, my friend? But that doesn't mean you're not a Russian spy, does it? FSB? Counter-intelligence? Economic Security?"

"I tell you nothing," Konstantin rasped, deliberately thickening his accent and turning it into basic Pidgin English.

"I don't like this, Lorenzo. How could the Russians know about us? Why would they even care what we're doing?"

Lorenzo? Konstantin recalled the name from the list of potential members of the Four Evangelists. Lorenzo Martedi: Italian history professor, Bible scholar, credited with the seminal theory that the Book of Revelation was a strategy for world domination. It made sense that he'd be in bed with Habersham.

One benefit of the sack over his head was that they couldn't see his face.

He waited.

"How did you learn of us?" Martedi asked, finally.

Konstantin said nothing.

"Why is your government interested?" Martedi pressed.

Again, his answer was silence.

"He isn't going to talk." Habersham sounded like a petulant child.

"He *will* talk," Martedi insisted. "Jonathan. See if you can loosen his tongue."

Ah, here it comes, Konstantin thought, bracing himself for the pain. Even though he had no idea what form the coercion would take, he knew it would hurt.

There was a loud *snap* and an agonizing jolt of pain burned into his thigh. Simultaneously, every muscle in his body went rigid. For a few seconds, his entire universe consisted of nothing but pain. He grinned through it. The one thing the big Russian could handle was pain.

"Careful," Habersham warned. Konstantin barely heard him over the crackling discharge of electricity. "You'll give him a heart attack."

The assault ended as abruptly as it had begun, and Konstantin sagged against his bonds, lactic acid draining away from his overburdened muscles. He felt a small measure of relief that his captors had elected to use this method of interrogation. There was nothing they could do to him that his KGB trainers hadn't done, more brutally, when he was young. He'd been shocked very nearly to death on several occasions as part of that training, and revived once with a defibrillator when it went too far. It would take a lot more than a zap from a spy store stun gun to break him.

Of course, he wasn't going to let Habersham and Martedi know that.

Martedi grunted unsympathetically. "Now, let's try that question again. Who are you?"

Konstantin panted dramatically against the fabric covering his face, making the hessian cloth suck into his mouth as he gasped, "Can't...breathe..."

The covering lifted just enough to expose his mouth and let in a sliver of light. "Who are you?" Martedi said again, like a broken record. "Who are you working for?"

"Karpov," Khavin gasped. "Anatoly Karpov."

"Who do you work for? The KGB, or whatever you call it these days?"

Khavin suppressed a smile. First, they didn't know their chess players, and second, they didn't know their intelligence agencies. While it was functionally still the same, the agency now went by the name *Federal'naya Sluzhba Bezopasnosti Rossiyskoy Federatsii* —FSB— and had done since the fall of the Soviet Union. "I saw you take him."

"Who do you work for?" Martedi repeated.

Konstantin didn't answer, and a few seconds later, electricity crackled through him.

Konstantin shouted through clenched teeth as the jolt subsided. "I was assigned to watch him. I saw you take him, and I followed."

"You were watching Pavic?" Habersham asked. "Why? Why are the Russians interested in him?"

The question was aimed at Martedi, but he focused on the name: Pavic. There was only one Pavic of interest: the man Habersham and Martedi had abducted was Kristijan Pavic, a former Serbian official, presently on trial in The Hague for crimes relating to the war in Kosovo during the 1990's. Now he was curious.

"I saw the flag," he ventured. "I know who you are."

Martedi's voice was salesman smooth. "Do you, now?"

"KLA. You are Kosovars. You know the World Court will acquit him, so you have decided to dispense your own brand of justice."

Konstantin knew this wasn't remotely the truth, he was giving them the chance to laud their superiority over him, and Martedi, right on cue confirmed it. "You see David? They know *nothing*. In fact, they believe exactly what we want them to believe."

Habersham remained unconvinced. "I don't like this. How do we know he's telling the truth?"

"It is the most plausible explanation," Martedi countered. "Relax, David. This is for the best. We were always risking exposure by using your villa. Now, there will be nothing to lead back to us. This is a good thing. Believe me."

Konstantin sensed that the interrogation was drawing to a close. He didn't want that. He had to keep them talking, keep them asking questions, otherwise he'd never learn anything. So he asked, "You... you aren't KLA?"

Martedi chuckled. "Of course not. There is no more KLA. But when Kristijan Pavic dies very publicly, the world will believe that they still exist. More importantly, Serbs will believe it."

Any satisfaction that Konstantin might have felt for tricking Martedi into making the admission was overshadowed by the revelation itself. So *that* was their game: a false-flag operation, designed to light the powder keg of latent ethnic hostility in the Balkan states. Not good. Not good at all. "Why?"

"The world has changed, my Russian friend. Last time, the Western nations came to the aide of the Albanians and gave them their independence. The Serbs haven't forgotten and they haven't forgiven. When Pavic dies a martyr's death, they will seek revenge. And who will help the Kosovars—the Albanian Muslim Kosovars?

"Not the countries of the West. They are sick to death of Muslims and their endless obsession with violence. Sick of sending their young men to defend, to *liberate*—" Martedi's

Italian accent amplified the contempt with which he spoke the word—"thankless, godless barbarians. They will wash their hands of Kosovo. And so it will fall to the Muslim world to look after their brothers."

Konstantin knew that the Muslims of Eastern Europe were as culturally far removed from their fellow worshippers in the Middle East as night and day, but if Martedi's prediction proved true, *if* the Western nations turned their back on Kosovo, it would be the final straw — damning proof that peaceful coexistence between the West and Islam was impossible.

It would mean war.

Not just random acts of terrorism carried out by extremists, but open war between nations.

The next world war.

"Why?" Konstantin repeated, no longer playacting. "Why would you want that?"

"It should not concern you. Your people stand to benefit, that is all you should care about. I've said more than intended." Martedi chuckled. "It is fortuitous that you stumbled into this. Perhaps your death at the hand of these barbarians will stimulate your politicians to enter the fray?"

Konstantin felt the hood tugged down once more, the last chink of light stolen by the brutal gesture. "Who is the horseman?" he asked.

There was a cold silence, and for the first time since waking, he could hear the muffled hum of jet turbines.

Habersham broke the spell. "Lorenzo? If he knows that..."

"He knows *nothing*." Konstantin felt hands grip his shoulders, and when Martedi spoke again his voice was cryptic, almost reverent. "'And there went out another horse that was red, and power was given to him to take peace from the earth, and that they should kill one another. And there was given unto him a great sword.'"

The hands patted his shoulders. "Soon, everyone will know the horseman."

Martedi had said all he was going to say.

The death sentence was par for the course, but Konstantin felt a new sense of urgency as he tested his bonds. His hands were cold and numb from the loss of circulation. There was no slack in the plastic zip-ties. Somewhere beyond the confines of his hood, the whine of the engines intensified. He heard the noise of wing flaps being extended in preparation for landing.

He breathed another curse.

He'd finally found the answers he'd been looking for, had grasped the true ambition of the Four Evangelists.

And there wasn't a damned thing he could do to stop them.

NINETEEN
SANCTION

Rome—0506 Local (0406 UTC)

Frost reacted instantly.

He threw himself flat on the floor.

He spider-crawled away, even as Denison's lifeless body pitched forward and what little remained of his face thudded wetly on the tabletop.

Heads were turning around him: the half-dozen patrons of the cybercafé had heard the crack of the bullet punching a neat hole through the window, but didn't yet understand what they'd heard. It would be a few seconds more before they realised that a murder had occurred right in front of them, and longer still to grasp why Frost was crawling around on the floor.

There was another *crack*. He heard it after a second hole appeared in the window: the difference between light and sound across distance. A sniper. Frost felt a pulse of heat and pressure as the round passed through the place where he had been sitting less than one second earlier.

He kept moving, angling closer to the wall directly below the perforated window, trying to get out of the sniper's line of sight as quickly as possible.

Long years of training had thrown him into a sort of defensive autopilot.

Keep moving.

Keep out of the crosshairs.

He'd worked out the angles almost reflexively; the shots had come from outside, probably from the roof of a building on the far side of the *piazza*.

Stupid! I should have made Tony take a seat away from the windows...

He shut down the part of his brain that was generating the recriminations. Self-flagellation was low on the list of priorities.

Keep moving. Stay alive.

Return fire.

Snipers didn't work alone. There would be a spotter, and in this environment, the spotter would need to be close to verify the kill.

He scanned the awestruck patrons around him without really seeing them. He didn't need to study their faces or gauge their reactions; he knew what he was looking for, and it wasn't here.

Outside then.

He sprang up from a crouch and hurled himself at the exit door, slamming it open and bursting onto the street. Frost immediately veered to the right, moving at speed.

There were only a handful of people in the *piazza*—a jogger, a few early risers out for a walk and a coffee before beginning the workday.

No one appeared to have noticed what was happening.

The sound of another bullet's impact ricocheted around him. He saw a spray of concrete chips as the round, pockmarked the cobbles of the pavement less than a metre in front of him exploded.

He spun around, changing course to prevent the gunman from filling him with lead, zigzagging with every few steps as he marked his mental map with the probable location of his attacker. Then he saw something else.

Several of the pedestrians saw his strange behaviour, but as in any public place, they made a visible effort to pretend they hadn't.

A man standing near the fountain stared directly at him.

He followed every move Frost made.

Frost didn't recognise him, but his dark blue anorak was very familiar.

It took him a second to place it: this was one of the men that had chased them through Kensington Gardens.

Frost looked away, hoping that the man hadn't caught the glimmer of recognition, and veered right, hard, running out into the *piazza*, before angling back to the pavement.

He repeated the manoeuvre again, closing the distance between himself and the spotter.

Then, when the fountain was only about thirty metres away, he broke into a full sprint.

The man's eyes widened as he realised what Frost was doing, and he reached under his jacket for a semi-automatic pistol.

He managed to bring the gun up.

Before he could get off a shot, Frost was on him.

They slammed together like rugby players in a ruck.

The man outweighed him by at least ten kilos, but Frost had momentum on his side. For the fleeting second they came together, that made all the difference.

His shoulder hit the big man's abdomen and sent him sprawling backwards into the fountain.

Even as he went down, the man managed to wrap his arms around Frost, pulling him with him.

Frost felt the chilly water close over him—bringing back the plunge into the flood trap below the *sacellum*—but with the added threat of someone trying to kill him.

They grappled like wild animals.

Any advantage Frost might have had disappeared in the face of his opponent's superior strength. He quickly found himself on his back, with the man's hands gripping his shirtfront, sheer, brute force holding him under the surface as he spat and kicked and tried to break free.

Frost struggled against the oppressive weight, trying to wrestle free of the man's grasp, but no amount of writhing or twisting helped.

He flailed blindly, trying to strike the man's face or chest, anywhere that might grant him a momentary reprieve from drowning.

It didn't help.

The blurry visage of his opponent continued to leer down at him, the hands that held him as unyielding as the roots of an oak tree.

As his initial primal fury began to subside, Frost knew that he'd underestimated this man, and his error was going to cost him his life.

The realisation was strangely calming.

Frost suppressed the aimless instinct to survive, and instead seized on the desire to *win*. It was different. Winning demanded a different kind of thinking. He stopped struggling; let his arms and body go limp beneath the surface.

His assailant wasn't fooled.

The man was evidently smart enough to know that Frost hadn't been under nearly long enough to have succumbed to asphyxia, but what he couldn't know was that the deception wasn't Frost's primary goal.

He was trying to focus on the indistinct face hovering above his own.

He stayed that way for several seconds, fixing his gaze on the man's lower jaw, and then put all of his might into a single punch that rammed like a sledgehammer into the man's chin.

The blow landed square, driving the man's jawbone up into his skull with a crunch that vibrated all the way to Frost's elbow.

The big man's head didn't snap back; his neck, like his arms, was thick with muscle and absorbed the energy of the punch, but his prodigious strength could not prevent Frost's fist from driving his jawbone straight back into the mandibular nerve cluster—what professional fighters called "the knockout button." Frost didn't believe for a second that his single punch had rendered the man unconscious—it would have been a million to one shot—but he felt the intensity of his opponent's grip relax, and that was all he'd wanted.

Frost seized the opportunity.

He threw his arms up out of the water and caught hold of the man's head, drawing it down to his chest, and in the same motion, twisted savagely as if he might, through raw fury alone, rip the man's head from his shoulders. Something snapped, a sound that reverberated through Frost's body like a gunshot, and the man instantly went limp, settling on top of Frost like a sandbag. A dead weight.

Desperate for air, Frost shoved the corpse aside and broke the surface, gasping.

For a moment, the craving for oxygen superseded all other concerns; but he didn't have the luxury of catching his breath.

He ducked down again, trying to use the bulk of the fountain for cover without knowing precisely where the sniper was hidden.

The towering figure of the merman partially eclipsed his view of rooftops. He felt exposed. Pinned down. He rolled over the concrete lip surrounding the pool and pressed himself flat against the warm pavement.

Frost saw the dead man's discarded pistol—a semi-automatic, equipped with a sound suppressor—half a metre away, and snatched it up.

He sprang to his feet and sprinted out into the *piazza*.

He didn't zigzag this time; doing so might have prevented the sniper from anticipating his movements, leading him the way a hunter leads a flock of birds, but it would also have increased the amount of time spent in the open, and right then it was all about time. The gamble paid off; no shots were fired.

Frost reached the front door seven seconds after crawling out of the fountain.

He burst through the door and found himself in a foyer with a flight of stairs directly ahead and an intersection of halls going left, right, and deeper into the interior of the building. Frost took the stairs, bolting up them two and at a time, the gun held out in front of him.

He narrowly avoided slamming into a woman coming down as he rounded the landing to the second storey, but he kept going.

A litany of colourful and decidedly unladylike curses followed him.

He didn't give a shit.

He reached the third floor, and kept going to the fourth.

One more flight of stairs continued up from the fourth storey landing, but the way was blocked by a chain that stretched between the handrails. Frost was just about to climb over the barrier when someone stepped into view at the top of the flight.

He froze in place and stared up at the man.

He was younger than Frost, but not by much.

Fit, though it was hard to be sure, since most of his upper body was concealed beneath a nylon windbreaker. His right hand was empty, but his left held the handle of a long, rectangular case—it was about the right size and shape to hold a guitar.

Or a rifle.

Frost saw a flash of recognition in the man's eyes.

And put a silenced bullet directly between them.

The man pitched backward and sprawled like a whore on the stairs.

The case slipped from his fingers and skittered down the steps, brushing past Frost. He made no effort to get out of the way. His attention, like the business end of the pistol, was focused on the landing above.

Five seconds passed. Ten. Thirty seconds. No one else appeared. The sniper had evidently been alone on the rooftop. If there were any more members of the hit team left, they weren't in this building.

Frost slowly lowered the gun and then turned and sank wearily onto the steps as the adrenaline tide finally began to ebb and the weight of what had just happened crashed over him.

He felt no satisfaction at having avenged his old mate's death.

Revenge wasn't a dish worth serving, hot or cold.

The skirmish was nothing but a coda: a bitter postscript to a long night that had ended with him accomplishing exactly nothing.

Denison had asked only one thing of him, and he had failed.

Tony was dead, the Crocea Mors was lost, and Lili was....

Lili.

Frost shot to his feet, clambered over the chain, and raced up the steps to the body of the fallen sniper. He rifled through the man's pockets, finding a pistol—the same model as the one he'd taken from the dead man at the fountain, and two spare magazines, which he stuffed into his pocket.

Then he found what he was really looking for.

He activated the man's mobile phone, and hastily punched in a number that was still fresh in his memory.

TWENTY
CONTACT

Nonesuch Manor—0411 UTC

It wasn't until the generic trill of the prepaid burner phone startled him awake that Sir Charles Wyndham even realised he'd dozed off.

His blood was a churning stew of caffeine and anxiety, but in the absence of information—it had been more than five hours since he'd last heard from Khavin—worry and stimulants couldn't stave off exhaustion indefinitely.

Lethe fielded the call, switching it over to speaker mode: "Hello?"

"Lethe, that you?"

There was no mistaking the voice with its Irish burr.

"Frosty!" Lethe almost shouted, his relief obvious.

The old man looked at him, thinking *Dear God, it actually worked.* "Are you all right?" Sir Charles asked.

There was a noise like a cough, or maybe it was a bitter laughter, that crackled from the speaker. "Not remotely, boss."

Sir Charles heard the weariness—the sense of utter defeat—in Frost's voice, and felt an overwhelming sense of grief. He'd done this to him. He'd left him out there, alone. He'd betrayed him. No matter the reasons, he'd left him to an uncertain fate, left him hanging in the wind, and while he knew of no one more capable, it in no way lessened his self-loathing. "I don't know where to begin, my boy, I'm so very—"

Frost cut him off. "I know. Forget it. Look, I think I know what's been happening, but right now I need Jude to do something for me."

"Name it," Lethe said.

"I need you to look up the list calls that went to my mobile, one of the last one's Denison's. I need to know the calls he made and received over the last few days."

"Roger that, Frosty," Lethe replied confidently. In fact, he'd already made that inquiry earlier in the evening at the old man's behest, hoping that it might provide some way of reaching Frost without alerting MI6. He brought the information up onto the wall-mounted plasma screens.

"What am I looking for?"

"Look for an overseas number, country code for Kosovo... or maybe Italy."

"Kosovo?"

"The phone belongs to Lilijana Pavic," Frost went on. "Right now I'm praying to every fucking heathen deity she was lying when she told me she didn't have one."

Sir Charles interrupted before Lethe could relay the number: "Ronan, there's something you need to know."

He took a deep breath, wondering if he had any right to heap yet another burden onto the man's shoulders. "I sent Konstantin to investigate Denison. He found information that led to one David Habersham."

"I know about Habersham. He's one of the Four Evangelists. Tony told me."

Sir Charles heard the spike of bitterness in his man's voice. He let it go. "Konstantin went to pay Habersham a visit at his house in the Netherlands—"

Frost cut him off. "The Hague! Kristijan Pavic's trial."

The deductive leap hit Sir Charles like a slap. "Jude. News reports from The Hague. NOW!"

"On it."

The computer display vanished from the plasma screens and was replaced by feeds from Reuters, BBC WorldWide, Sky News, and CNN International. Different faces were reporting the same news. The old man looked at the oldest, most dignified figure, trusting his white hair and elder statesman vibe, his eyes drawn to the graphic ticker running across the bottom of the screen: *Suspected War Criminal Pavic Abducted on the Eve of Verdict*.

So that's their game.

Or is it just the opening move?

"What's happened?" Frost asked.

"You don't know?" How was that possible? It was Frost's deductive leap that had directed them to look for this news. "Pavic was abducted from his hotel room."

Lethe supplied more details: "They killed the security team. No witnesses. Seems to have happened around midnight."

"Okay Ronan, is this what it's all about? Pavic?"

There was a long pause on the other end of the line. "No. Maybe. It's part of it, but...shit. I can't deal with that right now. Not yet. Jude, you got that number for me?"

Lethe glanced at Sir Charles, waiting for a nod of permission. The old man nodded. "I do. And to answer your next question, its GPS signal puts it in Rome."

"Pinpoint it. *Exact* coordinates."

Sir Charles sensed that Frost was about to sign off. "Ronan, there's more. It's Konstantin. He's...he hasn't made contact in over five hours—"

"Did you hang him out, too?" The words fairly smouldered over the line, but before he could defend himself from the barb, Frost continued, "I'm sorry. That wasn't fair. I know why you had to do it. At least I think I do."

"I'm not asking you to drop everything and go find Konstantin, my boy. Just take Denison and get somewhere safe until I can sort this out."

"Tony's dead." There was no anger in Frost's voice, only that same crushing weariness. "Lethe, I *need* those coordinates. Text them to this number. I have to go. The police are coming."

"The police? *Ronan*—" But Frost was already gone.

Sir Charles turned to Lethe. "Where is he?"

"Rome. Piazza Barberini. Only a few klicks from the signal he asked me to trace."

"He said the police were—"

"On it." Lethe busied himself at the keyboard. "I'm in the carabinieri network... of course, it's all in Italian, so... nope. There it is. He's right. Units have been despatched to Piazza Barberini."

"Do something to help him."

"Like what?"

"I don't know, and frankly I don't really care. Send them to a different street, change the description they're working from. Tell them Frost is working for Interpol. Just do something. Anything."

"Fine. But contrary to popular opinion, I am not a sodding miracle worker," he muttered.

"And send Frost what he wants."

"Already done."

The call hadn't relieved any of his anxiety. Frost was far from safe; Denison's fate underscored the seriousness of what Frost was still up against. And the news out of the Hague also added more uncertainty.

How were the Four Evangelists involved?

Why were they involved?

And what in God's name had happened to Khavin?

"Sir, I think you should see this." Lethe said. For once, there was no inflection in his voice. No excitement at having made a grand—impossible—discovery.

Sir Charles glanced over at him, and then followed his gaze to the images playing out on the plasma screens. The news ticker now read: *Extremist Group Threatens to Execute Hostages.*

A line of text indicated that the images on the screen were from a live webcam feed.

It could easily have been a still picture.

Two figures were seated in front of a large red flag, emblazoned with the double-headed eagle of the Kosovo Liberation Army and the silhouette of a scimitar crossed with an assault rifle. He recognised one of the seated figures as Kristijan Pavic. The accused war criminal looked lost, bewildered, as he blinked against the harsh glare of a camera light.

The man beside him, bound and gagged, was Konstantin Khavin.

TWENTY ONE
WHAT THE LIGHT CONCEALS

Location Unknown—0415 UTC (approximate)

Konstantin squinted, trying in vain to catch a glimpse of his captors.

He had seen nothing but the dark interior of his hood for... how long? Hours? Long enough for his eyes to become so accustomed to the darkness that the brilliance of the portable studio light felt like a red-hot poker being driven into his corneas.

No more than half an hour had passed since he'd come around. The plane had landed, presumably at some remote airstrip where no one would notice hooded and bound captives being bundled out of the cabin. He'd been transferred to a motor vehicle—a panel van, or a small lorry. The subsequent drive lasted no more than fifteen minutes. After that, he'd been moved a short distance to the place where he now sat. During all that time, he'd heard nothing more than the occasional hushed whisper, too soft for him to make out what was being said, and with his head covered, had seen nothing at all.

Then, with painful abruptness, everything changed.

The hood was torn off, and the blinding beam of an umbrella light that was brighter than the sun skewered him. A few seconds later, he heard a voice, speaking clearly—albeit distorted by some kind electronic device—in English, but the words weren't directed at him.

"Members of the United Nations and the so-called International Court of Justice: you have abdicated your responsibility to punish the crimes of the criminal, the butcher, Kristijan Pavic. You have failed to dispense justice, and so God has found you unfit to render judgement any longer."

Shapes gradually began to emerge from the haze of light.

There was another bound captive seated, slumped, less than a metre away from Konstantin. He recognised him as the man he'd attempted to rescue a few hours ago. Now he had a name to go with the face: Kristijan Pavic.

With each passing second, Konstantin could distinguish a few more details about his surroundings as his eyes adjusted. He was in an austere room with bare white walls and a concrete floor, the latter mostly covered with a sheet of black plastic. There were no decorations, aside from the enormous red flag, which Konstantin could just make out when he twisted his head. The only other furniture was a pair of folding metal chairs propped against the wall opposite the flag.

He and Pavic were not alone.

A figure dressed all in black—black tactical boots, black fatigues, black balaclava to conceal facial features—stood behind a tripod-mounted camera positioned alongside the studio light. Three more men, similarly black-clad, stood around the perimeter of the room, each with an H&K submachine gun slung over a shoulder. Konstantin didn't care about them right now. His attention was drawn to two men who weren't making an effort to conceal their faces. That fact guaranteed he wasn't going to walk away from here alive. It changed everything for him. It meant that there was no extra risk, no matter what he did. The end game would always be the same if he failed. One was David Habersham; the other, the man who had brought Pavic to Habersham's Dutch estate—Lorenzo Martedi. Konstantin noted that Martedi was watching the scene play out with an eager expression—bloodlust—while Habersham looked more like he was about to vomit.

Someone moved behind Pavic, another black-clad figure, whom Konstantin realised was the source of the monologue. "Now you shall see what justice really means."

Something flashed in the figure's hands—something metallic that reflected the light in just such a way that it seemed to be ablaze with supernatural fire—and was pressed to the side of Pavic's neck.

The Serb's expression remained confused, but showed no hint of fear.

Khavin knew that look.

Pavic was in denial; he still thought this was some kind of elaborate stunt, theatre that would end with some ridiculous political demands.

And then, with the first cut, his eyes came alive with horror.

A foul odour assaulted Khavin's nostrils—the iron tang of fresh arterial blood, the pungent ammonia of a bladder and bowels involuntarily voiding their contents. Pavic's mouth worked, but the only sound he could manage was a gurgle; the blade had already cut through his trachea. He didn't even clutch at his throat. The faint noise ceased as shock overcame the man, and then the merciful release of death.

Konstantin remained detached, mind racing. It would be too easy for panic to set in, aghast, transfixed by the horror of what he was witnessing. He couldn't let that happen. Even so, for a few seconds, he couldn't tear his eyes away from the gruesome spectacle of the dark-clad executioner sawing relentlessly through Pavic's neck.

Habersham rushed for the exit door, hands pressed to his mouth, chest and shoulders heaving.

Pavic's severed head hit the floor with a sticky, wet *thunk*.

Since waking on the plane, Khavin had known this moment was coming. There was a way out of this, there had to be; he just had to figure out what it was. Not bargaining, not pleading. Action.

I've got about thirty seconds to come up something, *he thought, wildly.*

He strained against the zip-ties holding his wrists together, but his arms were numb all the way to his shoulders, and the plastic ties dug into his wrists so deeply he was already bleeding. He couldn't tell if his extremities were even moving, much less if the bonds were loosening.

The executioner bent over, grasped Pavic's head by the hair—the formerly silver mane now streaked red, matted with gore—and displayed it to the camera.

"Justice is served," said the eerily distorted voice. "The butcher Pavic is dead. But you who sought to deny the people of Kosovo repayment of this debt have become sharers in his crimes, and now you also must face God's judgement."

The executioner let Pavic's head thump to the floor once more, and then moved toward Konstantin.

With a snarl, he redoubled his efforts to break free.

The executioner took a position behind Konstantin.

He felt a keen steel edge press into the side of his neck.

"This Russian agent was sent to protect Pavic," the executioner declared. "He will be the first to share the butcher's punishment. He will not be the last."

"Fuck you and your fucking mother," Konstantin Khavin rasped. "You're not taking my head."

A strange warbling sound issued from the electronic voice-masking device.

The executioner was laughing.

Konstantin planted his feet on the floor and pushed off as though trying to jump despite being bound. In the same motion, he thrust his head straight back, ramming the back of his head into his executioner's midsection. It was little more than a glancing blow, and accomplished nothing save to force the black-clad individual to retreat a few steps.

He was more successful with the second part of the desperate manoeuvre.

The chair tilted back on its rear legs, and then crashed to the floor.

The fact his limbs were numb didn't make it hurt any less as the full weight of his body fell against the chair's back, crushing his arms and pinning them to the floor.

He savoured the sensation; pain meant there was still a chance to wake his body up.

Konstantin twisted his body and kicked his legs out, rocking the chair madly back and forth as he tried to roll onto his side. If he could just break the zip ties, get his hands free, then he would have a fighting chance....

A fist slammed into his gut, driving out his breath and snuffing the guttering flame of hope that his act of defiance had roused.

As soon as he'd lashed out at the executioner, the three black-clad guards had moved in, swarming over him like piranhas in a feeding frenzy.

Another punch landed, and then another.

There was nothing he could do to fight back, no way to defend himself or lessen the impact of the relentless blows. They came in methodically, but with gleeful abandon. Again and again the three men pummelled. "Hit me," he snarled through bloody lips. "Go on you worthless sacks of shit. Hit me. Harder! Fucking harder!" He spat blood.

As the darkness engulfed him Konstantin felt a measure of relief.

He was going out on his own terms.

When the bastards took his head he wouldn't feel a thing.

TWENTY TWO
RED HORSE

Rome—0516 Local (0416 UTC)

"Come on! Move!" Frost yelled at the windscreen. He held the phone against the steering wheel, tracking his progress on its GPS map display as he half-wove half-crawled through the streets of Rome.

The early morning commute was already well underway, but every time he hit a major road the traffic moved briskly. It was only the narrow streets where things slowed down, because there wasn't room for two cars to pass at once. True to their reputation though, the Romans lived life on the edge without a care for their personal safety as they hammered their engines, treating the streets of the Eternal City as their personal Grand Prix track.

The biggest problem he faced was reversing his instinctive reflexes; the Italians, like everyone else in the world, drove on the wrong damned side.

Lethe had dumped the coordinates for Lili's mobile to his phone before Frost reached the car. There had also been an accompanying message: "The signal is stationary. I'll update you if it moves."

He hadn't had another text from Nonesuch.

The map showed the layout of the city. While Frost couldn't make out street names, which would have meant nothing to him anyway, he could clearly distinguish some of the city's more noteworthy landmarks—the enormous oval of the Colosseum; the serpentine curve of the Tiber River, snaking past to the west; and just beyond that, the distinctive outline of Vatican City. Even the *piazza* was easy to make out, situated just to the south of what looked like an enormous park.

His destination was not so well defined.

It showed only as a green dot, surrounded by a maze of lesser streets and narrow alleys, just beyond what appeared to be a railhead.

It was close, but since he didn't have wings, getting there meant following the circuitous roads of the one-way system marked on the GPS map with a green line that stretched from the dot to his own present location.

He bullied his way onto one of the main roads—*Corso D'Italia*—and then put the pedal to the floor.

As he'd raced from the *piazza*, he'd passed a police car, lights flashing and siren blaring, on its way in. It hadn't slowed or turned around. Frost's car was just one more anonymous Fiat on the road, but that would change as soon as bystanders who had witnessed his departure supplied a description of the car. Once that happened, the carabinieri would be able to isolate him using CCTV and traffic cameras and all of the tech Lethe would have used in their place. They would get the vehicle's license number, and then in short order, would have access to the car's GPS locator chip. In less than ten minutes, they'd have a helicopter in the air, watching every move he made, and relaying the information to ground units who followed at a safe and discreet distance. When he finally stopped, they would move in.

Frost didn't care about any of that.

His gaze flickered from the view through the windscreen to the display on the phone screen, and back again repeatedly.

He was only peripherally aware of the city now as it flashed by; it was an indistinct blur of sand-coloured shapes and dark verdure, all illuminated by the glow of street lamps and the approaching sunrise. He was focused on the green dot, the ever-shortening line that marked his route, and trying not to run into the car in front of him.

Frost veered south, onto the *Viale del Castro Pretorio*.

His destination was less than a kilometre away, just to the east of the thoroughfare, and with each metre that passed, he felt adrenaline surging in his extremities and pooling in his gut.

The green line indicated a turn. He whipped the Fiat hard to the left, ignoring the red light and the squeal of his tyres sliding across the asphalt. He couldn't ignore the fact that the entrance to the intersecting street passed through an arched opening in a high wall—a pedestrian bridge, or maybe one of the damned Roman aqueducts everyone was always talking about. The opening was wide enough for two lanes of traffic, but a cluster of red taillights clogged the arch and the street beyond. Unlike the boulevard, where traffic had moved like blood through an artery, this street was clotted with creeping commuters waiting on traffic signals and looking for empty parking spots.

Swearing, he jammed down on the brake, felt the car shudder as the anti-locks engaged, and felt the Fiat slow—but not nearly fast enough. He wrenched the wheel to the right, futilely looking for more room to bring the car to a full stop. There was none.

The Fiat fishtailed.

Frost was jarred violently as the wheels bounced up over the low curb, and was hurled bodily from his seat as the car smashed broadside into the wall.

He slammed into the door, his head crunching hard against the window.

He didn't feel any pain, not even from his wounded arm. That was probably a bad thing, but he was still conscious, and all his parts still seemed to be working.

The driver's side door was completely blocked, the immense stone wall pressed up tight against the fractured windows.

He had to climb across the seats to get out on the passenger's side.

He stumbled unsteadily onto *terra firma*, surrounded by a growing throng of concerned bystanders shouting at him in Italian. That single moment of culture shock rammed home exactly where he was and what he was doing. Frost stuck his head back into the car to retrieve two items, both of which had ended up in the foot well.

There was a gasp from the crowd as he emerged from the Fiat with the pistol, but Frost barely heard it. His attention was consumed by the display on the mobile phone. According to the GPS, he was .3 kilometres from his destination—300 hundred metres. "Out of my way!" He yelled, and charged through the arch, breaking into a flat out sprint as soon as he was clear of the traffic.

He knew where he was, but only because of the GPS: the campus of *La Sapienza Universita di Roma*.

Sapienza. The word literally meant *wisdom*, but Frost knew that what had begun here was not wisdom, not by any stretch of the imagination. It was madness.

Lorenzo Martedi, senior chair of the school's department of classical studies, had first proposed the idea of the Book of Revelation serving as a blueprint for world domination, and was in all likelihood, the chief architect of the Four Evangelists. Martedi had also been Lilijana Pavic's thesis advisor.

All the threads were tied to Martedi.

It was Martedi who had introduced Lili to the Path of Mars and to the modern *Salii* who kept the sacred relics and continued the ancient rites. It was Martedi who had given Lili the palimpsest, proof of the existence of the Crocea Mors, and had arranged for her to team up with Denison in order to track down that sword, all as part of his crazy scheme to unleash the Four Horsemen of the Apocalypse. The sword was only symbolic, not a prerequisite to the success of Martedi's plan, but what a symbol it was: the sword of Julius Caesar.

The sword of the War God himself.

It had never been meant for the rider of the white horse, the man who would be king. The Crocea Mors was for the red horseman, the living embodiment of global war.

The phone flashed a new message: You have reached your destination.

Not quite, Frost thought, glancing around.

From where he stood, he was equidistant from three buildings. GPS coordinates weren't pinpoint-accurate, but he was close.

Two of the structures were exactly what one would expect from a college campus, with students and faculty streaming through the doors for the first lectures of the day, but the third appeared to be undergoing a major renovation. Half of the three-storey building was covered in a tent of plastic sheeting, which hung from a skeleton frame of scaffolding. The only sign that the building might be occupied was the presence of a white panel van parked near the east corner.

Frost stuffed the phone in his pocket and hefted the pistol as he turned toward the van and resumed his sprint. Not for the first time, he wished he'd pressed Denison for details sooner. The size of the group that had been waiting in the subterranean vault: how many would he be facing now? Two? Four? Ten?

Again, he couldn't let himself worry about it.

He had the element of surprise, which would count for something, but no matter what the odds, there was no changing his side of the equation. There was only him—one man—against the tide. With a lot of luck, he would kill them all. Without that luck…well, he'd take as many with him as he could. He owed Denison that much.

He dashed up the front steps and hit the door without breaking stride.

It flew open.

He ran into a hallway with a lot of open doors—and one that was closed, to his immediate right.

He pivoted and launched a heel kick at the latch plate.

The door exploded off its hinges, and with the silenced pistol held out before him, he swept inside.

The sight that greeted him was not exactly what he expected, but the differences weren't enough to give him pause.

The room looked and smelled like a charnel house.

A decapitated corpse sat bound to a chair in the centre of the room, the severed head lying on its side in a spreading pool of blood. Despite the streaks of red that obscured the waxy countenance—the expression a frozen mask of disbelief—Frost recognised the victim, and the last piece of the puzzle fell into place.

Four figures, all clad in black, were huddled around another bound figure. Frost recognised this man, too, and felt a surge of hope.

Konstantin Khavin was still alive.

Barely.

One of his tormentors had a blade pressed against the side of his neck...a very familiar blade.

There were other details that flooded Frost's awareness; other men in the room, the camera on the tripod, the red flag that served as a backdrop. He ignored everything except the person holding the Crocea Mors to Khavin's throat.

He got the pistol up and took aim.

But before he could squeeze off a shot, something heavy crashed across his back and sent him reeling.

He sprawled into the knot of men holding Konstantin and rebounded, landing on his back as the object that had hit him—a folding metal chair—clattered to the floor beside him.

Konstantin's would-be executioner sprang into motion, leaping over the huddle, holding the Crocea Mors high.

The blade flashed, burning like sunlight, as it arced toward him.

Frost made a desperate grab for the discarded chair and brought it up to parry the killing blow. The impact vibrated through his arms as, in a spray of yellow sparks, the sword cleaved halfway through the chair. Frost held tight. The sword stuck there.

The executioner hauled back, trying to wrestle the blade free.

Frost also pulled, twisting the chair as he rolled away, and wrenched the hilt from the killer's grasp.

The executioner stared in dumb disbelief as the weapon was torn away from him. That little bit of luck. Frost's fingers curled around the polished brass hilt. With one hand still holding the chair, he yanked at the sword. It came free as if embedded in soft butter. It was hardly Excalibur out of the stone, but he wasn't complaining.

The Crocea Mors hummed in his grasp like a living thing.

Frost was on his feet, moving with a speed he wouldn't have thought possible.

It was as if someone had pressed the freeze-frame button on everything in the universe but him.

A machine pistol swung his direction, the muzzle spitting flame. The small room rang with the thunderous report, but Frost sidestepped the point-blank barrage. The Crocea Mors flashed, and the gunman fell back, a bloody geyser erupting from a gaping wound that stretched from his collarbone to his navel. It was a brutal way to die.

Frost slashed again, taking a second gunman, and then another.

He wasn't a swordsman. He'd never held a sword before, but it felt absolutely *natural* in his hands. As if he'd been born to wield the Crocea Mors.

He mowed through the gunmen, and in what seemed the blink of an eye, he stood surrounded by an array of hacked-apart human flesh.

Only the executioner remained standing, dazed and incredulous, backed up against the hanging flag.

Frost advanced, sword in hand, blood dripping from the blade.

There was nowhere for the black-clad figure to go.

The sword continued to hum in Frost's grasp, a siren song that burned through him like hunger...like lust. *Yes*, it seemed to say. *Just this one more, and I will be sated.*

He didn't need it now. He wasn't a murderer. The fight was over.

He let it fall to the floor.

The executioner let out a strangled whimper and took half a step forward, away from the wall, eyes locked on the blade. Frost blocked the way. His right hand seized the executioner by the collar. His left tore the balaclava away, releasing a cascade of hair.

He dragged the woman in front of the camera, letting the world see her face.

For a moment, he considered saying something to the unseen audience, to all those who had chosen to bear witness to this atrocity—

Here is your war leader. Your bloody *messiah*. Not a holy warrior; just a bitter, angry girl who was so ashamed of her father that she cut his fucking head off.

—but he stayed silent.

He held her there a few seconds longer, and then let go.

There were sirens in the distance; the police were coming.

He didn't want to be around when they came bursting in.

He retrieved the sword and used it to cut Konstantin Khavin free.

The Russian opened one eye groggily—the other was a swelling mass of cuts and bruises—and stared up at him. He'd taken one hell of a beating. "I didn't think you'd be the one to great me in heaven."

"Who said you'd go to heaven? Come on, Koni. On your feet. This isn't over yet."

"It never is."

*

The carabinieri, responding to reports of gunfire at the

university building, arrived on the scene ninety seconds later.

The two Ogmios operatives were long gone.

Only Lilijana Pavic remained, as unmoving as the dead that surrounded her, still staring into the unblinking camera eye.

TWENTY THREE
FALLOUT

London—0730 UTC

Sir Charles had always thought the old beech, Hyde Park's famous upside-down tree, looked like something from Tolkien. Instead of stretching up to the sun, the branches drooped low, spreading out on the ground like the tentacles of some ponderous Old Man Willow tree monster.

He came to the park as often he could, even now, when he needed Maxwell to push him along the paths. He refused to allow his disability to lessen the simple pleasures of life and the sensory feast: the sights, sounds, and smells of the park; the animals, the trees, even the visitors.

People were usually happy here, he could see it in their faces, and happiness was a contagious emotion.

His visits to this particular spot, however, were infrequent, and as a general rule, not at all pleasurable.

He'd sent Maxwell off and now he sat alone, his wheelchair parked alongside a vacant bench. He watched Quentin Carruthers—Control—stroll along the path toward him. Their eyes did not meet, but Carruthers casually approached and settled onto the bench beside him.

"Well played, Charles," he said, without preamble. "You not only saved your man—"

Sir Charles' hand snaked out and struck Carruthers' face. His open palm cracked like a gunshot against the other man's cheek. Carruthers rocked back, and one hand immediately came up to the offended area. A white handprint was visible outlined by a deepening red flush.

"Bloody hell! If you weren't a cripple, I'd—"

"If I weren't a cripple, I'd have rammed your teeth down your throat," the old man growled. "Remember that."

Carruthers glowered and caressed his cheek a moment, mastering his fury. "You're insufferable."

Sir Charles offered no rebuttal, and after a long pause, Carruthers spoke again. "I was only ever the messenger, you know."

The old man shook his head. "It didn't have to end this way. Frost could have brought Denison in, debriefed him, wrapped him up in a bow and kept the whole thing deep below the radar. That was the obvious play, and you ignored it. You *wanted* this to happen."

"This was a nasty business all around. You should know as well as anyone that there's no point in recriminations."

"No point? You assassinated the man, a public figure no less. You don't think that's going to come out?"

Carruthers glanced around. "Keep your bloody voice down, Charles. I told you, it wasn't my call. You're right. There, I said it. What more do you want? An apology? Fine. I'm sorry. But it's done now, we dodged a proverbial bullet. All's well that ends well, and all that."

"This hasn't ended, not by a long shot. We've only scratched the surface. Four Evangelists—four." He held up his hand, four fingers pointing skyward, to emphasize the point. Carruthers winced, as if expecting another blow. "Four parts to their plan. Four Horsemen, and what have we got?"

"We've got Habersham. Our men in Rome rolled him up. And we'll have Martedi soon enough. That's half of them. Their whole bloody plan was predicated on executing all four parts in tandem."

"And you don't think they'll try again? We don't even know who the other two are, much less what they were ready to unleash. Economic upheaval? We're a hair's breadth from that already. And God only knows what they had planned, what they still have planned, for the fourth horseman."

"We'll find out soon enough."

"I don't share your optimism, Quentin." Sir Charles took a breath, bringing his own rage under control. "My team got dragged into this, and that makes it my fight, now. We're going to hunt them down and see an end to it, and I don't give a good Goddamn who gets hit by the blowback."

Carruthers shook his head. "I can't let you do that. You've done a good job for us all…you saved the day and brought your man home safe and sound. You're a hero. Enjoy the moment and step back, let us handle this."

Sir Charles fixed the other man with a hard stare. "I wasn't asking your permission. In fact, I don't think I will need to ask you for anything ever again. I'm only going to say this once, Quentin: I'm taking Ogmios away from you."

"Like hell you are—"

"Consider it the price of my silence. You're right; there's nothing to be gained by recriminations. All the same, I shudder to think of what would happen if the world learned how *royally* you fucked up." He placed the emphasis on the word deliberately.

"Blackmail, Charles? How very uncouth." Carruthers scratched his head. "It won't work. Ogmios can't exist in a vacuum. Funding, intelligence…you're nothing without that. No matter what you might think, you're an extension of Six, and you don't get anything if you don't play by the rules."

Sir Charles waved dismissively. "Not anymore. Think of it as a divorce, and I'm the bitter wife. I'll claim alimony from Vauxhall. That will give us autonomy and resources, and you, dear boy, will be Control in name only. Those are the terms of my silence. Otherwise, I'll make sure you're finished politically, my friend. I'll end you."

"You don't mean that."

"Try me. And in case you get some bright idea about sending your bloodthirsty goons around to permanently change my mind, I would remind you that I employ a very talented young man named Jude Lethe, who can do the most wonderful things with computers. Everything's connected these days, or so he tells me. Everything's recorded by some camera or other in this city."

"Divorce." Carruthers chuckled mordantly. He got up. "A bit of advice, from one friend to another: watch your back."

Sir Charles Wyndham nodded. "One friend to another. Don't become another bitter old queen who doesn't realise when it's time to abdicate."

TWENTY FOUR
LIVE BY THE SWORD

Two days after, Westminster—1200 UTC

Ignoring the prominently posted 'No Parking' signs, Ronan Frost pulled the Ducati Monster to the curb in front of Clarendon House. He engaged the clutch and goosed the throttle. The 696 cc engine gave an animalistic roar, like a herald's trumpet announcing the return of a Knight Errant, and then fell silent as he switched it off.

Knight Errant.

He'd always found that term amusing. Although the literal definition described a knight who wandered on a quest—an errand—Frost had always thought it meant something different. A knight who'd made a mistake, an error in judgment, and lost his way.

He felt that he'd lost his way.

His own name—Ronan—sounded so much like *ronin*, the Japanese word for a rogue *samurai*, a *bushido* knight who'd lost his way. He had never really fit in; not on the streets of Derry, not in 1 PARA...and now, not Ogmios.

Sir Charles had explained everything, told him how Control had forced his hand and how he'd done everything in his power to throw Frost a lifeline, and now, of course, how he'd cut the team off from Vauxhall once and for all. But it didn't change the fact that for those few hours, he'd been set adrift...

He let go of the handlebars and dismounted stiffly.

Every muscle in his body ached, and the ache seemed to be getting worse with each passing day. The wound in his shoulder was healing without infection, but it was the car crash in Rome that had left him feeling like...well, like a car crash victim. He'd been popping paracetamol and codeine tablets like they were candy; they might as well have been, for all the good they did. Still, he'd come out of it better than Konstantin, who didn't make a good patient.

He shifted the heavy duffel bag slung across his back, and headed up the walk toward the front entrance of Clarendon House.

The Knight Errant, returning victorious from his quest.

It wasn't a good fit.

Tony Denison had been the one who'd bought into the notion of the knight's quest. Konstantin had told Frost about the letter, with its tacit promise of a knighthood. Frost had no interest in that. One Sir on the team was enough.

A cluster of Protection Service guards waited at the entrance, making no effort to mask their wariness, their contempt, as he walked towards them. They obviously assumed he was a bike messenger. Frost climbed the steps to the slab of carved marble that served as the porch of the royal residence. "Frost. I'm expected."

One of the men grunted, "Wait here," but made no move to announce Frost's arrival to anyone within the residence.

Frost leaned against the wrought iron stair rail, and crossed his arms.

He didn't want to be here, but in some strange way, by taking the sword, he'd also accepted the quest. He'd become Percival to Denison's Galahad. And now, like Percival, he was returning alone, albeit with one significant difference. Percival had only brought back the tale of the quest for the Holy Grail; Frost had the prize.

The doors swung open, and he caught the last few words of a heated discussion. He distinctly heard someone say: "I will not leave you alone with some Irish wanker," and then a voice, quiet but commanding, declared the matter closed.

A moment later, a man Frost could not help but recognise, strode onto the porch and gestured for the guards to wait inside.

They retreated through the door, but conspicuously remained just inside the threshold, watching.

In spite of his sour mood, Frost wondered if he should drop to one knee.

Instead, he pushed off from the railing and faced the man, inclining his head. "Your Highness."

The prince extended a hand. "Mr Frost. It is a pleasure to make your acquaintance at last."

Frost hesitated before he accepted the handclasp.

He was a soldier, and soldiers didn't shake hands with their superiors; but neither did they refuse direct orders from them. "Thank you for seeing me, sir."

"How could I refuse? I've heard all about what happened—or, to be more precise, what you went through. And I know that in a way, I'm partly responsible for it all. More than partly, I suspect. This was the very least I could do."

"Right. Well..." He stopped, the words deserting him. He was a man of action. He let others do the talking. He shrugged the duffel bag off his shoulders.

The guards tensed. The prince scowled at them and turned back to Frost. "Is that it? The sword is in there? The Crocea Mors?"

"Tony always meant for you to have it. But you do realise that it's not really what he thought it was. It was never the sword of Arthur."

The prince seemed unperturbed by the distinction. "Perhaps not in a literal sense, but in legend, the Crocea Mors, the sword of Julius Caesar, and Caliburn, the sword in the stone, are all one and the same. In this business, perception is far more important than reality."

Ain't that the fucking truth, *Frost thought bitterly.*

He set the bag on the ground and knelt to unzip it, but then stopped himself. "You know everything that happened? The Four Evangelists, and what they had planned?" He knew for a fact that the man did; Konstantin had confirmed as much. "You know," he continued, "that this was part of that plan. The sword and everything it represents...the authority to rule."

"I know of it now." A corner of the prince's mouth twitched into a nervous smile. "I was never involved, of course, and I certainly had no prior knowledge of their intentions."

"All the same, you do realise that by giving you the sword, we will be accomplishing one of their primary objectives. They'll have their white horseman."

This had troubled Frost greatly over the past two days.

The Four Horsemen of the Apocalypse were synonymous with calamity, but the identity of the first—the rider of the white horse—had always been unclear. Those who believed that Revelation was a prophecy of the End Times, were split on whether the white rider represented Christ, the King of

Kings—which was decidedly at odds with the malign nature of the other three horsemen—or if he instead represented something that only had the appearance of good. The latter camp often identified the white horseman as the embodiment of *conquest*.

In the philosophy of the Four Evangelists, the distinction was irrelevant: the white horseman was both king and conqueror. Their scheme had never rested on a foundation of opposing Manichean extremes; it didn't matter if the king was good or bad, only that he was in a position of power when the other three horsemen were unleashed.

In stopping Lili, Frost had thwarted the ride of the red horse.

They had meant for her to emerge as martial figure—a modern day Joan of Arc—avenging the death of her father at the hand of Islamic radicals, leading a sympathetic army of her countrymen in a new wave of ethnic and religious violence that would, from one small spark witnessed live on national television, become a wildfire burning across Europe and the Middle East. Lorenzo Martedi had groomed her for that role for more than a decade, training her in the secret traditions of the priesthood of Mars, even making her one of the Salial Virgins, who, according to some sources, had assisted the Flamen Martialis—the high priest—in offering sacrifices to the war god.

Lili had certainly done that.

But Frost also recalled his conversation with her in Saint Albans, how she had expressed utter contempt for her father's support of the NATO intervention in Kosovo. He suspected that, in her own twisted way, Lili was trying to redeem her father. If their ruse had succeeded, if the world had blamed Albanian radicals for the man's murder, then Kristijan Pavic would have died a martyr's death, and at last become someone for whom Lili could feel both pride and love.

Frost almost felt pity for Lili, though ultimately, her motives didn't matter. She had been permanently subtracted from the equation, but there were other variables, other ways for the remaining members of the Four Evangelists to make their mad vision a reality.

Lorenzo Martedi was still at large, and there was no way of knowing if he had other acolytes ready to step in and take Lili's place. The identity of the other two remaining Evangelists—assuming, of course, that their chosen name was to be taken literally—was also unknown.

David Habersham had reportedly swallowed his own tongue, bloated from cyanide, before interrogators could loosen it.

All of which meant that the Apocalypse Plan—as Sir Charles had taken to calling it—might still be extant.

If Frost handed over the sword as Denison had intended, would he be loosing the first seal on the scroll?

Could he take that risk?

And yet, how could he not? He owed as much to Tony. Moreover, he was a subject of the Crown; if nothing else, duty required it of him. The man before him had the blood of kings flowing through his veins.

It was a lot of responsibility for a simple lad from Derry.

As if reading the struggle in his eyes, the prince spoke again. "What would you have me do, Mr Frost? It's public knowledge that I have no ambitions for the throne. Possession of the sword won't change that, and it certainly won't make me, or anyone else who wears the crown, a sharer in this diabolical conspiracy. The sword is nothing more than a symbol of something that is already our right."

Frost didn't buy it. Power wasn't like that.

But then he'd never been much of a royalist.

He opened the bag wide, exposing the sword to the noonday sun.

The polished steel caught the rays and reflected them back like holy fire. He put his hand in, took the hilt, and felt the sword humming in his grasp.

"Actually, your highness, I'm not exactly here to give you the sword."

The prince cocked his head sideways, and then his eyes widened in alarm.

He started to turn back into the house, a cry on his lips, but before he could take a step, Frost lifted the sword from the bag. He held it up in both hands, the tip of blade pointing down, and then stabbed it into the centre of the marble slab.

There was an eruption of sparks.

A cloud of dust and smoke rose up around him, filling his nose with the smell of burning stone, but in his hands, the sword felt no different. There was no shudder of impact as the sword struck. The blade didn't skitter away, or gouge a furrow in the hard metamorphic rock, or snap in two, or any of the other things that a reasonable person might expect to happen. It simply kept going, as Frost had known it would, and when at last he let go and took a step back, he saw only the hilt and about ten centimetres of the blade; the rest of the Crocea Mors was imbedded in stone.

The Protection Guards rushed forward and surrounded the prince, their guns drawn and trained on Frost.

Frost let go of the sword.

He raised his hands.

The prince shouted for his bodyguards to stand down.

They didn't move.

Not immediately.

They seemed to sense there was still some sort of threat—one that they couldn't understand. Finally, the first of them relented and took a step back. Then, one by one, the men gazed at the sword protruding from the marble slab.

The prince approached the sword, his eyes bright, alive with an almost childlike eagerness. He reached out a hand and caressed the hilt.

Then he stopped.

Frost saw the man glance nervously over his shoulder, and knew exactly what was going through his mind. *What if I try to pull it out...and can't?*

Not my problem, Frost thought.

He turned and started down the steps toward his waiting motorcycle.

As he reached the Ducati, the prince's voice reached out to him. "Mr Frost!"

He stopped, but did not look back.

"I think we'll just leave it right there, shall we? Very symbolic. I rather like it."

Frost felt a chuckle building in his chest.

"I think that's a good idea, Your Highness," he called back.

Then he climbed onto the bike, gunned the engine, and drove away, the Knight Errant sent off to wander once more.

THE END

THE OGMIOS DIRECTIVE

Crucible
Steven Savile & Steve Lockley

Solomon's Seal
Steven Savile & Steve Lockley

Lucifer's Machine
Steven Savile & Rick Chesler

Wargod
Steven Savile & Sean Ellis

Shining Ones
Steven Savile & Richard Salter

Argo
Steven Savile & Ashley Knight

www.ingramcontent.com/pod-product-compliance
Ingram Content Group UK Ltd.
Pitfield, Milton Keynes, MK11 3LW, UK
UKHW021323180426
11947UKWH00017B/1395

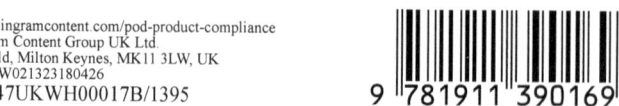